The African Girl
African Folklores

Justina U. Anumbor

WestBow
PRESS
A DIVISION OF THOMAS NELSON

Copyright © 2013 Justina U. Anumbor.

All rights reserved. No part of this book may be used or reproduced by any means, graphic, electronic, or mechanical, including photocopying, recording, taping or by any information storage retrieval system without the written permission of the publisher except in the case of brief quotations embodied in critical articles and reviews.

WestBow Press books may be ordered through booksellers or by contacting:

WestBow Press
A Division of Thomas Nelson
1663 Liberty Drive
Bloomington, IN 47403
www.westbowpress.com
1-(866) 928-1240

All scripture taken from the King James Version of the Bible unless otherwise indicated.

Because of the dynamic nature of the Internet, any web addresses or links contained in this book may have changed since publication and may no longer be valid. The views expressed in this work are solely those of the author and do not necessarily reflect the views of the publisher, and the publisher hereby disclaims any responsibility for them.

Any people depicted in stock imagery provided by Thinkstock are models, and such images are being used for illustrative purposes only.

Certain stock imagery © Thinkstock.

Publisher's Note: This novel is a work of fiction. Names, characters, and incidents are products of author's imagination. All characters are fictional, and any similarity to people, living or dead, is purely coincidental.

ISBN: 978-1-4497-8805-6 (sc)
ISBN: 978-1-4497-8807-0 (hc)
ISBN: 978-1-4497-8806-3 (e)

Library of Congress Control Number: 2013904368

Printed in the United States of America

WestBow Press rev. date: 04/02/2013

Dedication

It is very natural for me to dedicate this book to the only man who has had a tremendous influence in my life—none other than my father, Aniegbune Osadume. He was a pillar of strength in my growing years. He believed in me and prayed that one day a new dawn would break in the life of the little girl he had nurtured. My father gave up a lot to see his daughter grow into an enviable personality. The meager wages he earned did not discourage him from seeking the best education for his daughter. He was not rich, but he believed that the only thing that would make him rich was to give his child a quality education. He was right.

His dream was to see me elevated and above the children of those who mocked him while he suffered and searched for means to pay my school fees in secondary school. This book is released to mark ten years after he has gone to the Lord. He was a great writer and storyteller. His favorite story was the hunter and the only palm nut. Anytime I returned from school with low marks, he would whip me to remind me that I was different from the other children.

He told me stories of orphans who became kings, even when many odds were against them. If dead ones can see, I hope he can see that his little daughter has lived up to his expectations. Let him see the product of the many whippings I have endured under his tutelage. "I don't know how else I would pay you back, my dear father. Rest in peace."

Thy works shall praise you, O Lord, our God.

Ps. 145:10

Acknowledgments

To engineer Charles Ndubuisi Anumbor, my husband, for your wonderful support and unflinching love. To my children, Mrs. Sophia Ify Shofoluwe, Ogor, Ibe, and Charles Jr. To my grandchildren, Olaoluwatoni and Mope Shofoluwe, and my son-in-law, Olakunle Shofoluwe. I thank you all for your love and encouragement. May God bless you.

I also want to mention Shaunelle Page as one of those personalities that really motivated me to write this book for her loving care and endless attention to her three kids despite all the odds and the difficulties of being a single parent. I saw her working tirelessly to provide for the needs of her children. Regardless of her busy schedule, she found time to discipline and chastise them whenever they went wrong. I pray to God almighty that all your efforts for your children will not be in vain.

To all single moms and dads who believe in not sparing the rod and destroying the child, may you enjoy the fruit of your labor, in Jesus' name.

To that girl or boy who has refused to succumb to failure when faced with odds, remember that God has made you a champion. God bless you, and may you continue to shine, even above your contemporaries, in Jesus' name.

Table of Contents

Dedication v
Acknowledgments ix
Introduction xiii
Author's Biography xvii

Part One 1
    Ify 2
    Regina-Grace 8
    Lagos City 10
    Ify Goes to School 17

Part Two 27
    The Troubled Years 28
    Mama and the Pot of Egusi Soup 31
    The Uncrowned King 36
    The Scorpion and the Tortoise 39
    The Hunter and the Palm Kernel 41

    Onwuero 43

    The Coral Beads 48

    All of You 51

    The Beaded Necklace 53

    Why Men Have Catarrh 56

    Why Men Don't Have Tails 58

    Dike, the Great Wrestler 60

    A Dance in the Forest...65

Part Three 71

    A New Dawn 72

    Ify and Charlie 76

    Ify's Traditional Wedding..................................80

    Life with Charlie 88

    Disagreeing to Agree 92

    Ify's In-Laws...99

Part Four..105

    Ify Goes to America 106

Moral Relevance of the Tales..................................... 113

Glossary 117

Introduction
The Devil Is Gradually Harvesting the Youth of This Age

I have wondered at the great immensity and magnitude of moral bankruptcy in the modern-day world, especially among the youth. I have been a classroom teacher for close to twenty-five years, both in secular and spiritual education. I have come to observe a terrible drift that is moving faster than imagined in the way the youth of today are destroying their fathers' or mothers' legacies. There is no feeling of remorse or any kind or fear that could make them pause and rethink when they are determined to act against the rules and regulations in the home. They say charity begins at home. A child who has no respect for mother or father will do same outside the home. There is a serious drift today from normal to abnormal.

I have noted with trembling that the African society that used to be known as a primitive one is not left behind this horrible drift. The African society was known to be slow and sluggish. Today, the story is different. Children of African descent are highly rated in moral decadence. Tales by moonlight that made us shiver and tremble are treated with a wave of the hand by them today. The stories that revealed the philosophies and beliefs of the African people are no longer held in high esteem. The stories that shaped destinies of great men and women on the sands of time do not move them. The parents are not making things look good either. They have forgotten that the empire they are building will in one day be brought down by a child that is not tamed.

The Holy Bible has admonished parents to discipline their children if they really love them. The child they fail to discipline will discipline them in the future. "He who spares the rod hates his son but he who loves him is careful to discipline him" (Prov. 13:24). It is interesting to note that the society that has restrained parents from rebuking their children will at the same time help to dump them in the dungeon of their jail system in the future.

Children learn by stories. The children of Israel never forgot the stories of their ancestors' captivity in the land of Egypt. Yahweh specifically instructed, "Do not let this Book of the Law depart from your mouth; meditate on it day and night, so that you may be careful to do everything written in it" (Josh. 1:8). They were stories that were handed down from generation to generation by word of mouth. They recited them. They sang them. They rehearsed and acted them. They were meant to reveal the awesomeness of God almighty and give hope to the weak and downtrodden of the society. In the same way, the stories told in this book are meant to have the same effect in the lives of the young readers—to encourage them and to boost their morale.

I have selected these stories to serve as lessons to those children who desire motivation and spiritual upliftment. As a Sunday school teacher in children's ministry, I have witnessed that children whose parents attended church every Sunday or let's say who have Christian parents are not better disciplined than those whose parents are non-Christians.

My prayer is that all parents would stand and be responsible to the duty that God has given them, "for God will bring every deed into judgment" (Eccles. 12:14). They should live by example. I pray that every parent would learn to forgive their partner and live in biblical discipline and harmony, as ordered by God Almighty. If they did, society would experience less of the violence, anger, and hate that are slowly eroding the peace of these young ones. May God reveal the hidden treasures behind these myths, in Jesus' name.

—Justina U. Anumbor

Author's Biography

Justina U. Anumbor holds MEd French (University of Lagos, Nigeria); B.A.Ed (French), Delta State University; diploma, French translation (Montpellier, France); Diploma, LIFE Theological Seminary, West Africa (Lagos, Nigeria); diploma (basic), Children Evangelism Ministry, Inc. (Lagos, Nigeria). She is wife and mother. She teaches in the youth/children's department at Sure Foundation Ministries, Carrollton, Texas. She resides in Dallas, Texas, with her family.

Part One

Ify

She stood on the dock, and beside her was a gentleman who was supposed to be her father. He was in immaculate white trousers and a short-sleeved white shirt. He also had on white tennis shoes. He spoke in a known dialect. On the other dock were her maternal uncle, aunt, and grandmother. They looked very unhappy. "What is going on?" Ify seemed to be asking everyone. She was too young to understand. Justin had returned from the big city to claim custody of his only daughter. He had been separated from his wife five years earlier, and the woman had returned to her parents' home with their only child, Ify.

Life in the city had been very tough for Justin. With little education, he was able to get a job as a technician in the railways, where he had worked for over ten years. His uncle had told him about city life when he came home on vacation. Then plans were made for Justin to live with him and get a job. He had always prayed to go to the big city, so as soon as his uncle mentioned it to him, he was very glad. After Justin had worked for about five years, Ezuno, his mother, started bombarding him with the idea of picking a wife.

The first step was for Justin to move to his own private apartment, and this he did without wasting time. Justin had rented one bedroom in a home that was occupied by other families. He had planned to travel to the village that year to get a wife.

News had reached Ezuno—Nne, as she was fondly called—that Justin was playing the harlot in the big city. "The money he would have given me to build a mansion in the village, he was wasting it on city girls," Ezuno complained. She was very unhappy. She would give anyone she met who had come from the big city a letter to be delivered to her son. She had been warning him to keep away from city women. Justin had vowed to go home to get married. City girls were too wild for a man born and bred in the village. It was believed that these girls didn't respect their mothers-in-law and elders and were just too expensive to maintain. They attended wild parties and dressed flamboyantly, showing off their bodies like prostitutes.

Ezuno believed that a woman should be well bred, good natured, gentle, and obedient to the husband and to her in-laws. "Did you see what Nma was wearing? Her mother said she fries eggs and dodo every morning. In the afternoon, she eats chicken and rice; in the evening, she drinks tea and eats bread. How can such a wife know how to cook our traditional soup of *oseani*, *egusi*, and *agbona*?" she queried Justin. Ezuno had never seen any good in city girls. "If you see them in parties, they wear high heels, walking and knocking the ground; you would think these ones don't pass feces in the toilet," she lamented.

Ezuno had sent endless messages to her son that she had found a wife for him. Justin had agreed to come home at this time to meet with the family of the prospective wife of Ezuno's taste. Justin had saved just enough for this occasion. Both families would be meeting on Orie Day for the *igbankwu wanyi* or the formal introduction.

That morning, news had gone round to the entire village that

Justin had come from the big city to get married. Everyone was in jubilation because it was time for music, dancing, exhibiting new clothes, and plenty of *jollof* rice to eat. The men were more in jubilation because there would be plenty of palm wine.

Ezuno was in her best clothes. She moved from place to place, greeting the elders and the youth alike. Justin was in front of the building, entertaining his friends who had come to celebrate this happy occasion. At exactly five o'clock, the procession started moving to the bride's home. They were welcomed with pomp and pageantry. Everyone danced, ate, and drank. This was more of the adults' occasion. The youth stayed outside while the negotiation and introductions were going on. Then both families came to an agreement that the bride should come out and greet the husband's relations. The custom was for the woman to greet the elders on her knees. Her husband would be greeted last. The ceremony would be very brief. There would be announcement for dancing, after which the wife would be taken to the husband's house.

The days had been spent well. Justin had to return to the city with his new bride. Early that morning, a taxi cab had arrived to take him and Regina-Grace to the city. Amid tears and cries, they left. Regina-Grace had mixed feelings. She was a typical village girl, a bush girl who had never been to the city. Everything was strange to her, including this man. Her mother and Ezuno were friends. Ezuno had brought photos of her son to show to Nene, Gracie's mother, and the deal was struck. The fact that her son lived and worked in the city and spoke the white man's language, which was English, was enough attraction to woo Gracie. Gracie did not know the other side of Justin. The other side was very much unknown. She trembled as this strange man took hold of her left hand as they sat behind the driver's seat. She clung to her faith, trusting and believing in God.

Regina-Grace had a big responsibility on arrival. They lived in one bedroom, sharing the kitchen and bathroom with ten other families. She had to get up early in the morning. She prepared hot water, which she boiled on the kerosene stove. Next she had to get the right temperature by mixing it with some cold water, after which it would be taken to the bathroom. They had to take turns bathing. Sometimes there could be as many as ten buckets of water lined up, each tenant waiting for his or her turn to use the bathroom. As soon as it was time for Justin's, Regina-Grace would call, "Come on, it's your turn," in Igbo dialect.

Justin, with a towel round his waist, would walk into the bathroom. Breakfast must be served before he left for work. That was her daily routine. Sometimes Regina would go to work with him or stay in the company of another woman who lived far from the home, to babysit for her. According to Justin, other men could begin to look at his wife if he left her alone in the apartment. "You know, I don't really trust these women. Give them an inch, and they will take a mile," he told his friend Joseph as they played drought under the almond tree. Regina was a prisoner of circumstance. She was forbidden to mix with other women for fear that she would be taught "bad things."

Regina-Grace lived her life in intimidation and cruelty from her husband. She never would understand this man's nature. One minute he was the sweetest man, who any woman would be proud to have, and the next, he was beating and punching her like a bag. At last, after three years, God remembered her. She became pregnant.

Ezuno was the happiest. This was going to make her son more responsible. "These city girls have spoiled him; that's why he is always beating his wife," Ezuno told Baba. Baba was Justin's father, the village minstrel. He loved to tell stories to the children.

He enjoyed the brilliant light that shone through their eyes in bewilderment as they listened to him. He would sing and dance. That was how he won Ezuno's heart for marriage, according to tales. Baba had a sonorous voice; it would rise in a crescendo and then fall. He was loved by the villagers. What Ezuno did not know was the other side of Justin, the paranoiac nature that had turned him beastly.

The baby was born on Easter Sunday morning. Justin named her Ifeanyinachukwu. For the sake of this story, we identify her as Ify. The name meant "with God nothing shall be impossible." He adored her and watched over her like mother hen brooded over her chicks. There were now two women in Justin's stronghold.

Three months after delivery, Gracie received another battering of her life. Justin had seen her responding to a neighbor's good wishes for safe delivery. It didn't go well with him. The man had no right to greet or smile at Justin's wife; it meant there was something between them. Gracie pleaded, but it fell on deaf ears. She must never greet any man; that was Justin's verdict. Another day, baby Ify had crawled into one of the rooms, and Gracie had gone in to bring her out when she saw Justin coming from the passage. That was enough evidence for him that Gracie was the neighbor's mistress when he was gone to work. Gracie received another beating. She became very miserable and wished she had never met this man.

News flew to the village that Justin was about to murder his wife in the city. Ezuno shuddered at the thought of it and so decided to act swiftly. She arrived unannounced one evening and decided to take baby and mother back to the village until Justin became mature enough to handle a wife. Again, she blamed the city ladies who had bewitched her son for his inability to keep a wife. "When you come back to your senses, you will come and take your wife. I will not open my eyes and see you kill somebody's child in my presence," she said as she slammed the door of the taxi cab.

Regina-Grace

Regina-Grace was everyone's darling. She ran errands for all, both young and old. All the market days except Nkwo, she was in the farm, clearing weeds, planting seeds, or harvesting okra and melon. She was a great companion to her mother-in-law, Ezuno. She did all the cooking and washing. Early in the morning, she was at the stream to fetch water. Then she would go about four miles on foot to cut firewood. Everyone called her Gracie.

She did not have any education. All she could boast of was her feminine arts. She was a wonderful cook. She traded in palm oil when she was not on the farm with Ezuno. She was able to differentiate the different currencies in the money system. It was no problem, neither did it pose a threat in her trade. She was a disciplined woman.

Ezuno cherished Gracie, and every day she sent messages to her son to leave city women alone and come back for his wife. Justin was not perturbed. He liked his newfound freedom. He loved the city ladies. Suddenly Ezuno took ill and died. Regina had to return to her parents with her two-year-old baby.

Gracie was too young to be left alone without a husband. Twelve months later, her family gave her away in marriage to another man who was eligible. She left with her new spouse, while baby Ify stayed with her grandmother in the remote part of the village. Ify missed both her dad and mom in her young years. Night after night, she cried and cried. Ify slept in the day, and as soon it was nighttime she would burst into tears and cried till she fell asleep in the wee hours of the morning. No one could comfort her. This continued for over five years. Nothing gave her joy. She had a corner where she loved to sit and watch everyone pass. At the Otakara nursery school, she was very lonely. The oracle was consulted. The oracle requested the child be returned to her father.

A few months later, Dike, who was the custodian, received a summons from the high court to appear before the magistrate. The same notices were served to Adeke, Gracie's elder sister, and Nene, Gracie's mother. There was an uproar in the entire village. The court case went on for months to determine the right person to have Ify's custody.

Regina sent wired messages to her family that the child should be released to her father, Justin, but Regina's eldest brother, Dike, had refused. He wanted vengeance against the man who had dealt cruelly with his sister. He requested payment to offset all expenses incurred in the child's upbringing. He refused to let go, despite pleas. On the last day of the ruling, the verdict was not favorable for Dike and his family. Each of them was sent for three months of imprisonment, though with an option of paying a fine.

Justin walked across to the other side of the dock where Ify was. He held out his hands and carried her. He positioned her on his bicycle and rode towards his own village. His mission was accomplished. He would return to the big city the next day with his daughter.

Lagos City

The house number was 8 Igbobi Sabe Street. It was a one-story building. There were ten single rooms and probably the same number of families. Everyone cooked in the corridor or hallway. You simply placed the kerosene stove beside the door with a little cardboard as shield to prevent the wind or breeze from quenching the burning stove.

There were stoves made in China that you had to pump with all your might before the flame could become blue to cook meals. Woe unto anyone who was not able to produce a blue flame! The pots became painted with soot that took energy to scrub off. The second kind of stove was known as "senior service." They were the single types that had the kerosene tank on one side while the other was a double decker, which had the kerosene tank in the middle and two burners. There was no hassle to ignite these. All that was needed was to strike the match, lift the chamber, and light the fire. It would take about three to five minutes to get a blue flame.

What a spectacular sight it was to behold during the weekend. All the tenants would be in the hallway cooking. Different aromas filled the air. The most popular was egusi soup mixed with stock fish and bitter leaves. Agbona was another major soup with stock fish or dried *kano* fish. Sometimes if the dried fish was not properly washed, dead maggots would remain afloat in the soup. The young men who are known as eligible bachelors fried plantain or *dodo* with omelets. The young ladies paraded the hallway to and from their rooms, watching these young men do their cooking. It was very obvious that they sought for attention.

Ify and the other younger children would often make fun of them when at play. Nuru, the funniest of the group would say, "Ha, ha, ha, didn't you see how Brother Mike smacked Aunty Bisi's buttock?" And another would respond, "I even saw Brother Tony holding Aunty Nneka's hand." The whole group would burst out laughing.

Music filtered into the hallway from these bachelors' rooms just to attract the young ladies. They often listened to the Beatles or Sonya Spence or Cloud Seven. That was always a good time for the young group to make few pennies. The bachelors would often send them to deliver love notes to the aunties if their parents were at home. They should never be caught by their daddy or mummy or they would regret it. Once Nuru had been caught and had received the beating of his life. As he was handing the letter to Aunty Bisi, Papa came in. Nuru was compelled to do the talking. He ended with six lashes of *koboko*. Aunty Bisi on her part received extra vigilance from her mom and dad. She was never to be left alone in the house. After school hours, she had to stay with her senior aunty in the town, where Papa would come walk her home. She couldn't mingle with her friends anymore. She became a rare commodity, although her boyfriend never gave her up.

The children ran other errands for the older people in the compound. The strong among them went to fetch water from the next building. It was always hectic. There were plenty of free fights. Everyone wanted to outplace the other. It was chaotic. It took several hours before it would finally come to one's turn.

They loved every moment of it. It was time to abandon the dishes unwashed and for mother to take over. Sometimes the boys would leave their pails and go to another compound to play football with their friends. By the time they returned, the city would have stopped the water supply. They would return home with empty pails, telling their mothers that the water stopped running as soon as it came to their turn.

Mothers would believe these stories. After all, they were not there. Most times they hardly bothered since there was some water left for drinking. They loved to wash dishes for the young men because they had leftovers from their delicious meals. Their mothers served them *fufu* and soup. That was the most affordable staple food. Again, this meal kept them sustained for hours before the next one. The commonest was cassava powder, popularly known as *gari*. For very large families it was cheaper than fixing rice and stew or sandwiches or chicken or fish.

All the families suffered from poverty. Having sandwiches or rice or bread and eggs was a big-time luxury, which they could not afford. They believed that if children were served meat or fish, they were taught stealing. Meat and fish were for the elders. A good child should be contented with just eating the fufu, vegetable soup, and water to wash it down. At the end of each meal, she or he would be expected to say, "Thank you, sir or Mother, it was a wonderful meal." Any child who did not appreciate this kind gesture was termed as an ungrateful child and would be reprimanded. The children were very happy to have something to eat. Their mothers would remind them that there were many orphans roaming the streets wishing to be in their shoes and who would do anything to have these meager meals.

The young men didn't have many responsibilities. All they did was to spend their money on women, beer, and partying.

They could afford those delicacies, like fried dodo, eggs, chicken, and turkey. Uncle Segun was the most generous. They knew his fiancée, Tina. She was a pretty young undergraduate of the University of Lagos. She was always around at weekends. They would flock in Uncle Segun's room, just to catch a glimpse of this beautiful young woman. She loved to have kids around, even when her boyfriend chased them away. Uncle Segun would welcome her with a kiss on her cheeks. They would become excited and Nuru would mimic, "Eh e-eh-e-e-e," and the children would laugh. Outside they would mimic Uncle Segun and Tina. Nuru was a super actor. He would pick one of the girls, who would act as Tina. She would swing her hips in her dirty and torn dress. She swung her hips this way and that way, clutching her handbag. If she missed out any part, she was automatically fired and replaced by a better actress.

Majority of the children wore torn or dirty clothes. Only the rich could dress their children in short knickers, shirts, and slippers or sandals. Whenever they returned from school, everyone took off their uniforms and wore underpants or druses. The best they ever had was during the Christmas season. They walked about on bare feet, and it was by God's grace that their feet were not ripped by broken bottles or other sharp objects. Every one of them went to school just like that, without sandals or slippers. The only time they were finely dressed was on Sundays and partially for school. The poverty level was painfully high. But despite all this, they were happy and obedient children. Everybody was everyone's friend. It was a jolly compound. One's business was everybody's. They were very happy indeed.

It was a small community. Everyone minded the other's business. All the families knew everything about each other. One day a man came to the house when all the adults had left for work except for Uncle Segun. Nuru ran to his room to inform him that there was a visitor for Dandy. Uncle Segun welcomed and entertained him until Dandy got back from work. On another occasion, one of the bachelors was out of town when his mother visited. One of the families took her in for about two weeks until he returned.

There was no way to inform your relations about your whereabouts. There were no cell phones. The postal mail was sluggish. It was easier to appear physically than to go through the hassle of mailing letters, which normally would take weeks to arrive at their destinations. Every day they saw the post master or the mail man coming to deliver letters that had long being forgotten by the writers. He had on a big brown hat with a brown bag dangling from his shoulders. He had a pair of brown khaki shorts and a white shirt. Letters hardly came to number 8 Igbobi Sabe. He would walk from house to house delivering mail to the owners. He never smiled at the kids, even when they greeted. This earned him a nickname from them—*Tayintayin*, because he had a toothpick with him whenever he distributed the mail.

Igbobi Sabe was one of the dirtiest streets in the Lagos metropolis. Two huge gutters ran parallel with each other, with the main road at the center. On each side, there were houses of one and two stories painted in various colors, solidly constructed and with asbestos. In front of these buildings, there were dozens of makeshift kiosks of all sizes. Some were well constructed with wood, some with zinc or non-corrugated iron sheets. Beside the open kiosks, there were food vendors. There were women frying *akara, dodo, ewa, moinmoin, ogi,* and yam. No local edible was missing. Each vendor had her own charcoal pot, which was very close to the gutter. The gutter was not left out with its own mess on display. The rotten smell of food, dead rats, and roaches filled the evening air. Tadpoles and frogs leapt from one corner of the big gutter to the other. The nauseating stench from the dark water did not bother the sellers and buyers. They were more concerned with their take home. The vendors beckoned to passers-by for patronage. If one was buying from the food vendors, caution must be applied as one was standing on the wooden bridge so as not to fall headlong into the gutter. There were many of such bridges.

In the daytime, the city council would not permit such trading activities. As soon as it was four o'clock in the evening, there was a serious struggle to acquire a little space to commence their business activities. Commuters stretched their hands from their vehicles for purchases. Little boys lined up on the road sides wanting to do service for some of the passengers. Sometimes the bad boys collected money and scampered into the dark night. In other to checkmate them, the vendors gave them tips before or after sales. Sometimes they didn't take risks. They would rather use the devil they knew. The best way was to identify the compound they came from before they were allowed to serve. The tip was little, but it was better than nothing. It would be sufficient to buy puff-puff and buns at break time at school the next day.

The vendors had kerosene lamps attached to their tables. Some had the bush type of lanterns that burned with yellow flame and plenty of smoke. Electricity was a rare item at Igbobi Sabe. The people were used to living without it. The people's convenience was the lowest priority in the government of the day's agenda. It didn't stop the electrical company from passing out their bills at the end of the month. When there was light, it was compared to candle flame. Having an ice box was a rarity in the home. God bless you if you had an electric fan because it was rarely used. They depended on cross ventilation, which was hardly enough for the nine-by-nine-foot room with plenty children sleeping on the mat. Normally there was just one window, with mosquito gauze or net to keep away the buzzing aggression of insects.

The light bill had to be paid or there would be none for that period of time. If the children were fortunate to be awake when the city lights came on, one could hear a loud noise of jubilation. And if by misfortune it was taken away almost immediately, there was a big sigh of, "Huh, huh, huh, huh …" Such was life at Igbobi Sabe Street.

Ify Goes to School

Ify was up very early that morning. Justin had told her the night before that she was starting school. He had purchased for her a little school bag from the kiosk. In the bag were a plastic bowl that would be used for jollof rice at break time, a plastic cup and spoon, a Queen Primer, a pencil, and an eraser. She had a floral dress and a pair of plastic sandals. She was only permitted to wear those on special occasions such as today. Kids never wore shoes to school.

Ify was very happy. She walked proudly as her father matched behind her closely. She talked all the way like a parrot. Justin had told her that it was an all-girls school that had produced many intelligent women leaders in the society. The school had a convent where the reverend sisters lived. Sometimes they taught the children, Justin said. When they arrived, there were so many parents waiting at the gate, which was locked. They were seeking admission into the school for their children. Justin grabbed Ify's arms, lifted her, and sat her on the high gate, while the gate man stretched his hands, caught her, and set her on the ground. Justin followed almost immediately. It was survival of the fittest. In the next few minutes, they were both in the school compound walking towards the head teacher's office. The crowd behind them hurled insults at the gateman. They accused him of bribery and corruption. That was right. Justin had been there the previous day and had bribed the gateman. Their noise didn't make sense. The deed had been done. That was the game in the town.

There was a long line outside the headmistress's office. The atmosphere was relaxed. All the parents here were well dressed. They all spoke in English. The kids had their fingers tucked into their parents' hands. They all looked very clean. Later a teacher came out and gave out numbers on pieces of paper. Those were the admission tickets that would be needed to complete the registration process. They operated the free universal primary education in the region. A prominent politician from the defunct western region had promised the implementation of free education for all children. Everyone had voted for his party. The kids became tired of their temporary imprisonment and had to sneak away from their parents' claws to play. That was a welcome idea for Ify. The adults were in the line. Justin was there too. In a short time it was their turn. Ify had her photo taken and was given an inoculation and some papers were filled out. Justin did most of the talking and writing. One hour later, they were on their way home. They passed through a back gate and exited into the street of Saint Agnes.

The next day was Sunday. Justin didn't go to church. Ify had to follow another family to Saint Dominic Catholic Church. That was the only Catholic church in the neighborhood. It was a big parish. The reverend fathers and brothers lived there. There were Fathers Clapperich and Dailey. People loved Father Dailey. He made the congregation laugh. There was always a huge crowd any time he administered the mass. He had some funny things to say to the children. This Sunday, Father Dailey was the officiating priest. All the children were quiet as the sermon went on. Then it was time for the communion. There was perfect silence. One could have heard a pin drop on the floor.

Ify whispered to Aunty Iyabo, "What's going on?" She tapped her again to ask why there was silence. Aunty Iyabo put a finger across her lips, signifying silence as she pushed her head further downward. "Aunty, Aunty … Aunty, are we hiding from God?" Ify inquired. *Something must be the matter,* she imagined. At the end of the mass, she wanted to know from whom they were hiding. "Who owns that plenty, plenty money in those bags?" she asked Aunty Iyabo about the offering. The story did not end there. She thought Justin would have an answer. Yes, Justin knew everything. The "money was very big," she said as she narrated her story to Justin later that evening.

Monday arrived. Ify woke up very early. She carried her bowl of water and entered the bathroom. There was no line yet. The bathroom odor made her puke. The entire floor was slippery. She had to be cautious. Normally, Ify would have chosen to take her bath in the backyard when it was still dark. But on this day, there was light. The city had given them light. She hurriedly bathed and jumped out of the slimy floor of the bathroom. She was as clean as she could be. Justin was awake when she entered their one-room apartment. She put on her new uniform and no sandals. She loaded her new school bag with different items. There were three exercise books—2A for English, 2C for arithmetic, 2D for writing, and a drawing book.

The way to school was a long walk. Ify was equal to the task. Sometimes she ran and then walked to be able to catch up with Justin's strides. Her first day at school was going to be a memorable one. She was very excited. She longed to meet with new friends, see a new environment, and see her new teachers. All was new. Her score on the placement test put her in primary 1A, and that was supposed to be for kids with high scores.

Ify met with challenges that would build and shape her life forever. The language spoken was different from her dialect. At break time, no one wanted to play with her because she didn't understand them. She kept to herself most of the time. At break time, she lined up with the other pupils to buy food from vendors. Ify had hidden her one penny in her pants, so when it came to her turn, she dipped her hand inside her underpants and tendered the money to the food seller. The vendor gave her some yam porridge that was hardly enough to feed a two-year-old. She sat in a corner and ate her meal, drank some water, and returned to the classroom. She placed her head on her desk and fell asleep. Noise from all corners indicated that the break was over and it was time to start lesson.

Ify was a brilliant child. With the language barrier, she could still beat all her classmates in all the subjects—arithmetic, English grammar, comprehension, composition, nature study, writing, art, music, civics, history, geography, and literature. She was an excellent pupil. At the end of every session, she won the first prize. This, of course, didn't go well with the other pupils and gave them more reason to isolate her. She was not bothered.

Ify successfully completed her elementary education after five years. She gained admission into the secondary school in another state. Ify was an excellent pupil. Justin was thrilled by her performance. Ify became the talk of the town. She topped the list in the National Common Entrance to Secondary Schools. She was awarded a scholarship for the first year. With the first-year fees out of the way, more money was needed to do other purchases. It was a boarding school.

Justin had no money. He had become very restless. He had

promised his only daughter the best education. He told her that he had no property for her to inherit. After all, his father died a pauper. Justin had been to many places and different homes of his rich relatives, but no one could loan him some money to put his daughter in school. Justin said that one of them told him, "You don't have money and you allowed your daughter take the exam to an expensive school." He was only a technician with the railways. His salary was hardly enough to feed his family. Moreover, their wages were always three months behind. Before it arrived, it was used to service his past debts. They had often lived from hand to mouth. Justin knew the only way to get even with the rich in the society or with his rich relatives was to educate his daughter. He believed in her. He trusted her. He knew Ify would not put him to shame. Anyway, they still had three months before school started. He was going to try his hand at something different—something he had wanted to stop in his life and something that Gracie and his mother had spoken to him about giving up.

The English season was on. He stubbornly walked into the nearest pools office to gamble. That was his last resort. No one had the right to deny his daughter an education. That was his topmost priority. He staked four numbers on the coupon and submitted all the pennies in his pocket. Justin had to beg for food for himself and Ify. He didn't care. This business had to be taken of. Justin wasn't given to church, so he didn't know about Holy Ghost's fire to consume all obstacles and hindrances in the way of winning the jackpot. He only believed that his daughter would go to school. Nothing would stop it. He had believed.

One week had passed no news. Justin was devastated. When he was alone, Ify could hear him talking to himself: "No way, I say she will go, no, she will go …" Meanwhile, Ify had told everyone who cared to listen that she was going to school. Justin had lost all appetite for food. The only happy person was Ify. She dreamt of her new school. She lived in euphoria. She would demonstrate her new style of walking, how she would behave in the dormitory, and how she would respond when her superiors called her. Oh, she was in a different world altogether. Her father churned and burned as he waited patiently for the English season to come to an end.

Just one month before school was to resume, a stranger came to visit Justin. It was the local pools manager. Justin was given a slip. News like this had to be delivered personally. Justin had won the jackpot—five hundred pounds! After he had opened the slip, he asked the stranger if he wanted tap water. The ice box in the house had not been turned on for two weeks because of the lack of electricity. The stranger declined and only invited Justin to come to their office the next day.

Justin looked up into the sky, and with both hands raised, he said, "Thank you, God. Thank you for the day you gave this child because I know you will take care of her. My Father, this child will not disappoint you in her journey in life. Amen.

"Amen," he said again as Ify walked into the room. Justin blessed her by placing his hands on her head. *What is going on?* she wondered.

Justin announced to her that they would be going shopping the next day. Ify didn't believe what she had just heard. She didn't sleep the whole night. News went abroad that Justin had won the jackpot and that Ify was going to the reverend sisters' secondary School.

The school list was bought to the letter. Justin was fulfilled. He paid for the remaining four years of the boarding school so that he didn't have to worry again. He told his listeners that his dead mother gave him those numbers he had staked. He was very proud of his achievement.

Our Lady of Apostles Girls' Secondary School was privately

owned by the Catholic diocese of the state. It was a little boarding school with about three hundred students. There were about a hundred student boarders in the hostels. The school was located on the outskirts of the city. Within the school premises was a convent for the reverend sisters to the left from the main entrance gate, while the church was at the right. The Catholic church had a little parish. The officiating priests lived here. It was evidently smaller in size compared to Saint Dominic, although there were not many fathers or brothers living there.

The fathers were very kind to the students. They seemed to like the senior girls most. They were big and very busty. Every night they returned late to the dormitories, especially when the matron was not home. The juniors didn't know what was going on. Those senior girls who spent most time there said the brothers taught them math. These seniors were very nice to everybody, and they always looked forward for them going to spend time outside the dormitory whenever the matron was away. They usually returned with lots of candies and chocolates.

The matron, Mrs. Boyo, was very strict. She managed the four dormitories. She was tough on the senior girls but very nice to the juniors. She was a grandmother and had seen a little of the world. She spoke very good English and always had her hair in a ponytail. Some girls said she was mixed breed because of her very light skin color. There was another group of senior girls and these were really bad. They ill-treated the juniors. They borrowed their money and would never pay it back. They took their provisions and would never return them. On weekends when Mrs. Boyo went to her family, they were out all night. Smoking was not very common among these girls. But every weekend they went into the town and returned with all kinds of clothes, high-heeled shoes, exotic perfumes made in Paris, London and Milan, brassieres, pants, chocolates, cookies and candies. No junior girl knew their business but every time they looked forward to their return, because sure enough, there would be lots of free gifts for everybody. No one had the courage to report to the authority for fear of intimidation or any kind of reprisal from their classmates. It was none of their problem though, the kick-backs was what mattered to the junior girls.

One Saturday morning, the boarders woke up in the midst of commotion. There was pandemonium everywhere. All the seniors were seen gathered in the principal's office. Their faces looked grim. All the junior girls were ordered to stay in their rooms until instructed to come out. There were sirens all over the premises. The crowd was growing bigger. All the teachers were there. Mrs. Boyo was in tears that could be seen from the distance as she constantly wiped her face. Something terrible must have gone wrong, because after that day, Mrs. Boyo was never seen again. Some said she was transferred and others that she was fired from her job. Anyway, another woman took over her position. Later news had it that a senior girl had birthed a premature baby on the ground-floor toilet. This was discovered by the housekeeping manager, who had alerted the principal. Mrs. Boyo was ashamed that in spite of her harshness such could happen under her care. She had to turn in her resignation. That week, many of the senior girls were expelled.

The boarding school had four dormitories, which were located on the third floor. There were Our Lady of Monica, Our Lady of Sharron, Our Lady of Lourdes, and Our Lady of Apostles, known as the school house. Ify was in the school house, which had about thirty girls, and so did the other dormitories. Ify had always wondered why it was called a grammar school. The school offered arts subjects, most sciences, except physics, music, and home economics. English language, literature, biology, and mathematics were her favorite subjects.

She kept to herself. Every morning, the school bell woke them up at five o'clock for the students to get out of bed, and get ready for the morning mass at six o'clock. Fifteen minutes before the hour, students would line up on the assembly ground to be marched to the chapel by the prefects. Mass usually ended at quarter to seven, and then it was time for morning duty, which entailed cleaning in whatever location was apportioned to the student. At quarter to eight, the bell would ring for school devotion, which was led by the school's senior prefect, chapel, and the house prefects, including the principal and the teachers on duty. After prayers and announcements, the students would march into the classrooms. There were only two arms of each form. For instance, form one would be one-x and one-y, two-x or -y, and so forth. Ify was in Form one-y.

Ify chose a school mother. She was called Senior Irene. All the junior students in first form called those from year two to the last grade "seniors." Woe betide the junior girls if they ever called their seniors by their names without that appendage. It meant a lot to them. Senior Irene loved Ify so much that she would do anything for her. She protected Ify from the bullies among the other senior girls. Ify, on the other hand, had to make sure she collected Senior Irene's meals from the cafeteria every time she was not in the dining room.

The seniors were the "authorities" in the school. They lorded over the junior ones mercilessly. The juniors were their errand girls, washed their clothes, cleaned up their closets, and picked up their meals from the cafeteria. On Saturdays, juniors were compelled to braid their hair free of charge at the expense of their study hours or prep. The juniors dared to complain. When Ify was promoted to form two, she had the opportunity to retaliate on her juniors, but something in her would not allow her. She had compassion on her juniors and continuously appealed to her classmates not to maltreat them.

Ify was favored by everyone. She was intelligent and went on her way. She never insulted her seniors and did errands whenever possible without complaint. She was very serious about her academics. Once in a month, Justin paid her a visit, bringing her provisions like corned beef, sardines, corn flakes, powdered milk, sugar, washing soap, and other toiletries. They were not much compared to what other parents brought for their daughters. Some parents brought jollof rice, stews, chicken, fried fish, fried meat, and porridge. The meals were very tasty. They looked very colorful and sent irresistible aromas that lingered in the dormitories the whole weekend. If you were not in that student's good book, you would be left out in the sharing of the free gift. One continued to imagine how the food tasted. Most times Ify would decline their invitations because she would never be able to return the kind gesture.

When there was a fight between the girls, Ify heard them exchange horrible words. They would describe some foods as being awfully salty or overcooked or salt-less or spicy or tasteless or very watery. Some would say that the other's mother needed to be retrained in a catering school. Those outbursts made her sad. But amazingly, the next day, Ify would find these girls walking together after airing their dirty laundry in public. Ify wondered if that was how all rich girls behaved. Because of this, she never liked to have any of them as friends. She knew how much Justin had labored to have her school fees paid. She was not like the other girls from wealthy homes. She had entered the school on merit. More importantly, she didn't have a mother who would cook all those delicacies. It was just Justin, an old railway worker who struggled to make ends meet. The fact that she had come in here was miraculous. It was a great privilege and the breaking of a new dawn for a poor African girl.

Part Two

The Troubled Years

Justin and Ify had shared troubled times together. Gracie had left, and Ify's entire life was with Justin. Father and daughter had become inseparable. Justin had referred to Ify as the only palm nut in the fire. Ify thought that life was very cruel because her mother was never there for her. Therefore, the bond between daughter and father increased day after day. Ify remembered a particular night when she had gone to sleep hungry on her torn mat on the floor. There was no food. Justin had managed to give her *gari* soaked in water with a pinch of salt for breakfast that morning. Gari was cassava flour that had only carbohydrates. If it was made into a paste, then it would be served with vegetable soup.

She always knew when times were hard. Justin would be talking to himself. In the middle of the night, he would hum softly his favorite tune: "My God delivered Daniel, my God delivered Daniel, my God delivered Daniel, why don't you deliver me?" That was a signal that things were really, really bad. Ify would be withdrawn, and she accepted whatever she was offered for a meal. She would go into nearby bushes and cut some wild vegetables. Justin chopped them in pieces, washed them in clean water, and added some palm oil, water, and crawfish and put it to boil for a few minutes. Ify gladly accepted the meal with thanks. Rice was eaten only on very special occasions.

When the railway workers went on strike for nonpayment of their wages, there would be no food in the home. Justin would cleverly send Ify to their neighbor's to assist with house chores in order to have a meal for the day. She was only lucky if the meal had not been served before she got there.

The neighbor was from Justin's hometown. He had a wife and nine children. He worked in the railways like Justin, but he was the locomotive engine driver. Each time he travelled to the northern part of the country, he returned with plenty of food. The first daughter was Ify's classmate. Her name was Pattie. She was very spoiled. She had a boyfriend in the elementary school who gave her money. Pattie had told Ify that the man was her uncle. Anytime Ify followed her to his bookstore, Pattie would ask Ify to go buy some biscuits in a nearby store while she waited for her. Whenever Ify returned, the uncle would give them three pence and requested Pattie to come the next day. On the way home, Pattie would ask Ify not to mention this to her mother. Both of them shared the money equally. Ify spent hers on pork meat. It tasted so delicious. Ify always looked forward to accompanying Pattie to the uncle's bookstore. When they quarreled, Ify would lose the chance of eating pork meat for that time. Ify was smart to tolerate Pattie's excesses as much as possible or she would go hungry. Pattie could ask her mother to send her away. Pattie was not Ify's match in academics. Pattie's parents openly mentioned that they wished Ify was their child.

Justin was very proud of his only daughter. On days when the house was dry, Justin compensated by telling her stories. Every night they would sit at the patio overlooking the street. Justin sat on the recliner while Ify sat at his feet, facing him. It was a full moon. He told her stories of their origin and ancestors. He also told stories of the tortoise and the elephant. Ify liked them. She would invite her friends at school who lived nearby to come listen to these folktales. The elders admonished the youth through moonlight stories. They were lessons that were relevant to the society at large.

According to Justin, all the animals could speak at creation until this privilege was taken from them by Olisah, the Almighty. Justin said they also lived in homes just like humans. She wondered how the little tortoise was so smart that the elephant was always losing out in contests with him.

She recalled those many moonlight tales. She loved them so much and wondered how these would impact her life. She smiled as she remembered the story of mama and the pot of egusi soup. It is prepared from melon seeds. These are rich in oil and cholesterol. The soup is often prepared for dignitaries and special occasions. It is expensive to make and demands expertise and skill to come out rich and tasty. It is served with cooked plantain or any form of carbohydrate.

Mama and the Pot of Egusi Soup

"All things work together for good to them that love God, to them who are the called according to his purpose" (Rom. 8:28).

Mama counted all the items she had purchased from the big market to be sure that the sellers had not cheated her. Sometimes she had paid for some foodstuffs but when she got home, she discovered different items. She learned her lesson the hard way. She was not going to make that mistake again. She had purchased fourteen items. She carefully set them on the kitchen table and started to put them up in the cupboard. "Ah, this child, where is he to come and assist me?" she said.

Bomboy, on hearing mama's steps in the hallway, had vanished into thin air. He was not ready to go fetch water for cooking. At this time of the day, the tap was usually filled with kids from all the neighboring villages. Some went there just to fight. Some came to finish their quarrels at school. The tap was their meeting point. The boys had their short knickers on, and the girls had a piece of cloth tied around their chests to cover their developing breasts. The big girls wore dresses.

They had formed a long line. Each was carrying a pail or a large basin. This was where the big boys met their first dates. The big girls never fought but separated the junior ones from striking each other. Sometimes, if it was in the evenings, the big boys and the big girls moved away from the noisy kids for talk. Eighty percent of the young men in the village had met their partners at this particular center. Mummy and daddy never scolded or talked rough to them when they stayed longer than necessary or brought water late to the house. The villagers had often laughed at Iyabo, whose mother told her to stay longer at the tap so she could get a suitor.

Bomboy had escaped to the field to play football with his mates.

"Bomboy, *Bomboy!*" Mama shouted.

"Okay, you will come back and meet me in this house," she added.

That was the usual thing. She had borne Bomboy during menopause, after she had given up all hope. But she had spoiled him beyond repair. Bomboy at fifteen had no human feelings for his mother. Since he realized he was the only child, he had become so bad. Nobody in the entire village could scold him. When Teacher Adafor wanted to discipline him at school, Mama knelt down and would rather receive the lashes of the cane than for Bomboy to be beaten.

"Adeeke, this boy will kill you one day if you don't handle him well,"

Diokpa scolded his wife. Well, the boy refused to change. Bomboy had grown wings and was well above discipline.

Mama washed all the dishes, cleaned her son's mess, and prepared to cook soup. She had bought *egusi* (melon seeds) because

Diokpa had requested it. Mama usually asked what soup to be cooked. If not, she would be in trouble. Diokpa had a mistress who he gave certain allocation of his farm's proceeds monthly. She lived in another part of the town. She menaced the men with her beauty and endowments and tormented the women with her audacity. When Diokpa argued with Mama, he sneaked out there for his meals.

Mama hated this woman with perfect hatred. Anytime the woman met Mama at the marketplace, she would deliberately get closer to her to greet her. People said she wanted to see the anger in Mama's eyes. She used to be the village beauty in her younger days. Life had dealt bitterly with her. Her husband died during World War I, and she was childless. Stories had it that she aborted all her children while she was growing, and when the time came for her to have children, there were none left in her womb. Strangers would turn around to look at her twice when she walked past. Age had added grace to her beauty. She was a seasonal catch. This time it was Diokpa's turn. She was hated by all the women living with their husbands. Adele was a serious threat to Mama. Mama had often wept over the day the woman met Diokpa.

Mama searched for the large pot and set it on the stove, which was made in China. She hissed, saying to herself

"What am I going to do with this boy? How can I call my own son and he won't answer me? *Na wa o o.*"

She cut the vegetables and blended the tomatoes with some peppers. She poured three cooking spoons of palm oil into the pot. Next she added the chopped onions. An irresistible aroma permeated the air as the onions sizzled in the hot oil,

"*tjarrah ah, ah a ha aa*" as it continues to sizzle in the pot. There was a little disagreement but mama was undaunted. She continued to stir the mixture as if nothing has happened while they gradually came to terms. She lowered the flame, then, she stretched her hand to lift the blended ingredients of red tomatoes, red bell peppers and garlic. She aimed slowly at the bottom of the pot as she poured the contents into the frying condiments.

"Tsch, tsch, tsch," immediately the sizzling stopped to embrace a new powerful hissing sound as the mixture joined the frying onions. She stirred it for the last time before placing the lid over the pot.

"Jesus is the sweetest name I know," she hummed to herself while she cleaned the cooking area where oil had splashed. The battle between the heat from the stove, the pot, and the condiments had just begun. The blue flame burned with great intensity and aggression. The pot was at her mercy, and there was no resistance. The paste responded with immediate alacrity and hopelessness. The lid wished to counter the coup, but the large handle held on tight with a warning: "You dare not leave me alone…but how can you do that?" The lid answered in anger, "…sorry, I am out of here!" And then there was a bang! Mama looked toward the raging flame, moved expertly to the cauldron, and applied pressure on the lid, making it tighter. "You see, I told you," said the pot to the lid." "Okay, you win!" the lid replied, and there was quiet for two minutes before another form of bombardment unleashed.

Again, Mama lowered the flame and added ground crayfish, about a handful. She stirred the ingredients. She glanced at the wall clock. Diokpa would soon be home from work. She hurriedly added the ground melon seed (egusi) and stirred slowly with the wooden spoon. Skill was needed at this point if she wanted to make this soup palatable. She would not want to stir vigorously so as not dissolve the egusi balls. She carefully lifted the entire pot, shook it from side to side, and returned it to the stove. With the eye of an eagle, she watched keenly for the slightest sign of burning.

Now the whole kitchen had assumed the expected aroma. Mama's mouth salivated, and her stomach growled with hunger. She kept watch over it for the next ten or twenty minutes. The condiments knew that all hands must be on deck to make egusi spring forth its eggs with grace. Egusi commanded authority. At last there was harmony and unity in the old big pot. Mama turned off the flame and dished out a wonderful soup. She has won Diokpa's heart for the next few days, and she smiled!

Let us pray: Oh Lord, let the glory of my destiny shine out in Jesus' name!

The Uncrowned King

"Blessed is the man who does not walk in the counsel of the wicked or stand in the way of sinners or sit in the counsel of mockers" (Ps. 1:1).

A long time ago, there lived a man and his wife with their only son. The man's name was Iweka, and the woman's name was Adeke. The little boy's name was Elue. Iweka was the obi of the town. Everyone came to him for counsel. He was a wise man. People loved Adeke because she was humble. Elue did not take after his mother or father. He started frequenting the village square at age twelve to drink with the adults. None dared stop him because he was the obi's son. He graduated as the first in his class in *ogogoro liquor(local gin)* and palm wine. He told his fellows that when he became the obi, he would promote them as high chiefs. When he became an adult, women flocked around him because they said he was the heir apparent to the throne. Elue refused to acquire training in the traditional education of his people. He rejected farming, hunting, or fishing to prove his capability as a potential ruler. He refused to attend the usual meeting of council of elders where he could learn some wisdom. He was always found anywhere there was new wine exploits. He dressed in chieftaincy regalia and paraded himself as the chosen prince.

Iweka was unhappy. He turned to Adeke and laid the blame on her. Iweka proved himself a success in his kingdom. He settled every dispute in the land. Those who came weeping in any suit returned with joy. He was the people's man. If he called one chief, many responded. When he called his own, no one came. He was despised in his own home by his son. Not quite long, both man and wife became old and he died out of grief. Adeke could no more help in the situation she found herself.

And the people of the town wanted a new obi. It was the tradition not to mention the death of the obi until a new one had been crowned. The chiefs in council were afraid to mention Iweka's death to Elue for fear that he would run his mouth in the public square. Adeke was taken away by the elders out of public eye. Elue did not know what had become of his father and mother. They only told him that they had undertaken a journey to the next village and would be away for seven market weeks. Oliseh the oracle had denied Elue as the new obi to be enthroned when he was consulted.

It was a task for the council of elders and the chiefs to elect the obi for the town. Names were compiled, and everyone was requested to be in the village square on the last market day for the coronation. Elue was happy; his dream had come true. He ordered the best palm wine in the land and beyond. He and his friends arrived amidst pomp and pageantry, with music. He did not stop to find out what had become of father and mother. "Oh God of mercy, deliver us from such a child,"

Justin said, and everyone present echoed, "Amen."

The votes were cast. Elue was tricked by the lord of Bacchus, and instead of voting for himself, he put his friend's name. This friend emerged the winner, and Elue lost. Emeka was favored by the gods as the new obi of the town. There was great rejoicing.

Elue never saw his mother or his father. He swore to take revenge against those who hated him including the gods. None of his friends had the courage to tell him the truth. People said they saw him wearing a crown made with sticks on his head and others said he was seen in the market square dancing naked with a keg of palm wine clutched under his arm. Any time the children saw him they sang and clapped behind him and asked him to dance for them. They would tease him saying, "Prince dance, dance for us the kingly dance, just as you would when you become the king…" and he would start after which he would be given a penny. And so, four weeks after the coronation of the new obi, Iweka was laid to rest. Nobody knew how Adeke ended but she never saw Elue any more.

"That is the end of my story," Justin declared.

Let us pray: Oh God of heaven, deliver me from the power of peer pressure that wants to destroy me, in the name of Jesus.

The Scorpion and the Tortoise

"All her friends have dealt treacherously with her,
they are become her enemies" (Lam. 1:2).

Many, many years ago, when only the animals ruled the world, there were no human beings. There lived the tortoise and the scorpion. The tortoise was called Mbe, and the Scorpion's name was Akpi. They were very good friends but only from a distance. When they attended the village meetings, they supported each other when it came to casting votes on certain decisions affecting them. It was a common knowledge that these two were very good friends.

One day the animals in the village wanted two representatives to attend a conference in another part of the kingdom on their behalf. Mbe and Akpi were unanimously elected. The journey was to take them across the ocean. Mbe proudly told the chief animal that he would be glad to carry his friend Akpi and swim across the mighty ocean to the venue of the meeting.

The day was fixed, and both set out for the journey. They travelled a day's journey through the thick wilderness, hand in hand, sharing each other's meals, singing, and dancing. They slept in turns at night so as to ward off any danger or attack from other unfriendly beasts. Soon they arrived at the shore. Mbe offered his back for Akpi to ride while he swam across the big ocean. Halfway into the water, Mbe received a terrible, hot sting on his skin.

He yelled, "My friend, what are you doing stinging me? Oh, that hurts real bad! No, no … no …" He shook off Akpi from his back.

Akpi cried aloud, "My friend, I am sorry, that's the only thing I know to do well. Oh help, I am drowning!"

But Mbe could not be pacified as he swam away from his poisonous friend and returned to land. Akpi drowned, and his body washed to the shore!

"This means you must watch who your friends are because some of them might be absolutely dangerous and wicked," Justin concluded.

When Justin lifted up his head, half of the crowd was asleep. The mothers called each child by their names and asked them to go home. *That was weird,* Ify concluded.

Let us pray: Oh God, by the power that has made you God, separate me from unfriendly friends and miserable comforters, in Jesus' name.

The Hunter and the Palm Kernel

"Have I not commanded thee? Be strong and of a good courage; be not afraid, neither be thou dismayed for the Lord thy God is with thee withersoever thou goest" (Josh. 1:9).

Story, story, story. Once upon a time, time, time, time, the hunter Anene had just returned from the forest. He had not caught anything. All the animals had vowed to stay out of human trouble. That night the big and the little animals had gone into hiding. Dawn was approaching. He had trekked a long distance into the heart of the forest. It was time to return. His head lamp had gone out. He looked for his miracle charm, chanted some incantations, and the next minute he was in his little hut. His father had given it to him and asked him to use it when he was faced with danger in the forest or if he got lost.

He took off his hunting bag and hung it over the fireplace. He was hungry. The only food available in the hut was a palm kernel nut, which he had picked from the village square. He lowered it into the fire amidst the ashes and watched it cook. After a while, he picked a fork and searched the ashes for the nut. He didn't find it. He searched once more, but he didn't find it. He went toward the door to see if anyone had come in when he used the latrine. The door was securely locked. He was baffled.

Hunger bit him harder. His stomach growled as in the battlefield. His intestines churned in anger. The leftover oil from last meal in his large intestine started to melt. His vision became blurry. "Lord, help me," he muttered. He decided to empty the ashes into another area of the fireplace. He separated the light chunks of ashes slowly, and behold, there it was, sandwiched between two rocks of black charcoal. He salvaged it and threw it into his mouth. That was a good meal, and everyone laughed.

Let us pray: Empower me never to give up, even when the odds are against me. Oh Lord my God, answer me by fire, in the name of Jesus.

Onwuero

"Honour thy father and mother; which is the first commandment with promise; that it may be well with thee, and thou mayest live long on the earth" (Eph. 6: 2–3).

Everyone loved the story of Onwuero. It's been told many times. Each time it was told, it was better than the previous. The tune was beautiful to hear.

In those days, there lived a very beautiful girl. She had a father and a mother. They were a happy family. Onwuero was an eye catcher and was tall and pretty. She always wore her wrapper around her waist and another around her breasts. Around her waist, she had beads of different colors. Both ankles also had some beads. Whenever she went to the river to fetch water, she was an object of admiration. People thought she was a marine goddess. She was outrageously beautiful. Strangers in the town lined up just to look at her. Her hair was jet black and very long. When you looked at her eyes, you would think they were swimming. Men were very afraid to ask for her hand in marriage. They just believed they were not good enough for her. The prince, whom all the villagers thought was interested in her, decided to go to a neighboring village for a wife. The men who were courageous enough to approach her were turned down. She complained that they were too short or too skinny or too fat or too poor. There was always a reason to reject the suitor.

Onwuero became miserable. "I don't want to be an old maid in the village. Get me somebody," she said. Her mother consulted with all the village oracles, but none could provide a suitor. She offered sacrifices to their dead relatives—perhaps they could be appeased—but nothing happened. So one day, her mother became ill and asked Onwuero to help with her merchandise in the next flea market, which took place weekly. She was delighted. It was a good opportunity to navigate a strange land. A day before the market day, Onwuero had put finishing touches to her hair with braids, her wrappers were neatly folded, and there were beads to adorn her waist, ankles, and wrists. As she walked on the dusty path to the market with the pot of palm oil on her head, the birds were singing, but she did not care to pause for a second to understand their counsels. The message was:

Onwuero, when you see, pause, my sister,

Onwuero, when you hear, pause to think,

Onwuero, the world is wicked, Onwuero.

The village flea market was not an ordinary one. Stories had it that ghosts bought and sold there. In fact, the village carpenter had seen his dead sister selling some merchandise. Immediately after he set eyes on her, she vanished with her items. The carpenter had returned to the next market day, but he never saw her again. (Justin then added that the sister had gone to a distant flea market, where she would never be recognized.) Every market day, there was a fine gentleman from a distant village who frequented it. He was very handsome to behold. He was tall and always had a smile for everyone. All the market women always accompanied their daughters with the hope that this gentleman would stop by their stalls to do some purchasing, but he never did. Mama had forgotten to advise Onwuero that there was something sinister about this gentleman.

Onwuero walked confidently into her mother's stall, aware that all eyes were on her. She managed to put on a smile here and there as people greeted her. No sooner than she had settled into her mother's corner than this gentleman arrived. He had the most bewitching smile. His teeth were very white. His eyeballs were dazzling and very beautiful.

Onwuero was hypnotized. She had never seen a beautiful man like this. She took the hand extended to her and invited the stranger to come in. Within minutes, the whole pot of oil had been sold. Onwuero counted the money to make sure she had the correct amount. She thought her mother would jubilate. Now it was time to go. The stranger bade Onwuero farewell till the next market day. Onwuero offered to escort him a few yards before returning her own way. The stranger agreed. The walk meandered through the entire market until they finally came to the end of the square. The stranger bade her farewell, but Onwuero pleaded,

"No, let me escort you a little more."

"Okay, just a little," the stranger said.

They went another fifty yards and stopped.

"Go back home, young lady. My home is far," said the stranger.

"No, I want to follow you, please," replied Onwuero.

They continued with this drama for the next few miles till it was nightfall. From nowhere, a voice called the young man:

"Barracuda, give me my wrists. You stayed so late."

The stranger said,

"Oh, I am sorry. Here they are, thank you."

He unhooked the wrists and gave them to the owner. In the next mile, another voice cried,

"Eh, Mr. B, where are my arms?"

The stranger unplugged the arms and returned them to the owner. In the next mile, another deep voice queried,

"When are you going to give me my legs?"

The young man disconnected them and handed them to the owner. Now the stranger had only thighs, a head, and a neck. His voice changed to the sound of the deep.

Onwuero was stupefied. Her mouth remained opened all the while, and saliva got stuck in her throat, so she could not cry. She continued to follow the stranger like a zombie. All the borrowed parts of its body had been returned. There was only a massive fish on the ground, hopping and twisting in the manner of big fish swept ashore. The stranger-turned-fish had a deep, evil voice. He was no longer sweet. He growled at her,

"It is too late to return, my dear. My home is in the deep, and that is where you belong."

Onwuero, then remembered her mother and burst into this song:

Onwuero n'aba ... samala
Onwuero n'aba ... samala
Anyi bi n'ogbu ... samala
Ogbu bu miri ... samala
One gbu n'egbu (2ce)

Azu ewen re ' uno (2ce)

Imakwa n'a asa nwa asangwo, n'azu ko bu ... samala

Imaka Okpor nwa okpor ngwo n'azu ko bu ... samala

Imaka eke nwa isi achara nazu ko bu ... samala

Onegbu, n'egbu, azu ewen ro ' uno

Elosi m ilolo, okwu ilolo agwu n'obi, samala, samala, samala

The massive barracuda jumped into the air and hit Onwuero with his tail, knocking her into the ocean. Onwuero screamed,

"Help, help!" but there was none. The fish dragged her, and both disappeared into the roaring waves. They were never seen again.

The floor was filled with young sleepers. Justin cleared his throat and asked the mothers to take away their sleeping children, while Ify bade them good night. There would always be tomorrow.

Let us pray: My Father, my Father, my Father, deliver me from the principalities and demonic powers and the evil rulership of this environment in the name of Jesus. Oh Lord, open my spirit eyes to see beyond the ordinary eyes. Empower me to discern, and grant me the wisdom to choose right, in Jesus' name.

The Coral Beads

"A sound heart is the life of the flesh: but
envy the rottenness of the bones"

(Prov. 14: 30).

A long time ago, there lived two friends, Olu and Ayo. Olu had a beautiful, coral-beaded necklace that he loaned Ayo for his daughter's naming ceremony. Ayo had earlier loaned his miracle pot to Olu to help secure his pear tree that was under siege from the village goats. All the goats would not allow the tree to grow. They wanted it for food. When Ayo finally suggested that his miracle pot be used, it was a great idea that worked wonders. All the animals stopped eating it or coming near it. It suddenly grew into a mighty tree, and it bore golden pears. Olu became very rich when he started selling the proceeds of the tree. It had a lot of fruit each season and brought in much wealth.

Ayo became jealous. The little that Olu gave him was not sufficient. He wanted Olu's pear tree or else … Ayo could not be appeased. He grumbled all day. He started to speak evil of Olu in the village square.

One day Ayo rose at dawn to visit Olu. He wanted his little pot back because he needed to sell it so as to make some money too. Olu begged him, saying there was no way he could get the pot out without destroying the tree. Ayo would not listen. He wanted his pot or nothing.

Edumare came down from the sky. He begged Ayo to be reasonable. Ayo refused. He wanted his little pot. He had his way. The pear tree was cut down, amidst tears. As the tree was falling, the pot was broken. Ayo didn't mind. He bent over and picked the broken pieces. He would have rather had it destroyed than to see his friend flourish.

Some years later, Ayo's daughter, Ewa, was ready to get married. All the villagers gathered to wish her well. Ayo was very excited at the occasion. He had invited people from all walks of life. On the morning of the ceremony, Olu emerged from nowhere. Olu had turned grey and was beyond recognition. After the pear tree was cut, he had decided to leave the village. Now he had returned to claim his coral beads. The beads looked radiant on Ewa's neck. The beads had been sown together and had brought her good luck everywhere she went. They were miracle beads. They had carefully grafted into her skin. It was impossible to remove the beads without causing injury to Ewa.

All the renowned surgeons in the land were called to operate on Ewa to retrieve the necklace. It was impossible to do it without killing her. All the herbalists in the universe were summoned, but there was no solution without killing Ewa. Ayo became afraid. He looked to the right, but nobody spoke. He looked to left, but there was no friend to help. Sleep wandered away from him too. Olu would not receive any price. He wanted his coral beads.

"You know the rest of the story," Justin said sadly as he rose from his recliner.

Let us pray: You sun, the moon, the stars of heaven, hear the word of the Lord. I decree and I prophesy, my destiny will not be cut short, in the name of Jesus. Evil covenant entered into by my ancestors, I command you to break in the name of Jesus. I will not pay for what I do not owe, in Jesus' name. Amen.

All of You

"Lo, this is the man that made not God his strength, but trusted in the abundance of his riches, and strengthened himself in his wickedness" (Ps. 52:7).

In the olden days, all the animals lived together and shared things. The tortoise was very friendly with Nza, the sun bird. One day, news came that Almighty was having a huge party, and all were invited. The animals decided to attend in a big way. They all made new clothes. The journey was going to take seven days before they arrived the destination in the sky.

Mbe, the tortoise, was most excited. He summoned all the animals in the king's palace. He said that it was an opportunity to prove to the Almighty that there was great unity among them. In the meeting, he told them that they should assume new names, since it was a special occasion. They all agreed. Everyone chose different names, quite different from the usual. Mbe the tortoise chose the name, "All of You," the dove chose, "Cuckoo, Cuckoo," and the parrot would be called, "Master of Ceremony" or MC for short.

On the appointed day, all the birds donated their feathers to lift those who didn't have means of flying. Mbe had a ride, including other land animals. They flew for seven days and seven nights nonstop. It was actually a world conference. The living and the dead were in attendance. Mbe and his friends sat in a group. Then it was time for entertainment. Almighty asked the MC to announce that the served food was for *All of You*. He did as requested. Mbe grabbed the heavy bowls of rice and emptied them into his back sac. Nobody challenged him. He smiled wryly at the other animals. He was happy. He rubbed his chest and ate some of the food and did not think of sharing with any of his friends because the food was only made for *All of You*; they should wait for theirs.

The time came for the drinks to be served. All different types that no one had ever seen were placed on the table. Almighty instructed the MC, "This is for all of you." MC passed all of it to Mbe's table. When the conference ended, everyone left. Mbe's group was the last to leave, thinking they would be served, but Almighty had given all the food and none was forthcoming. This group of the animals was very angry. They decided to withdraw their feathers from Mbe. Mbe was left alone in the sky. Everyone had gone. The clouds were starting to fold away as the storm was on its way. There was nothing to hold Mbe. He fell and fell and fell and fell no more. As he was falling, all of the food splashed to the Earth and sprung as mangoes, oranges, tomatoes, and the rest of the citrus trees that we have around. Mbe found himself in the deep, and he decided to stay there forever out of shame. That's why there are so many sea turtles.

Let us pray: By the power in the blood of Jesus, Father, empower me to see what you suffered for me on the cross of Calvary, and help me not to cause pain to my neighbors, in Jesus' name.

The Beaded Necklace

"Behold, I send you forth as sheep in the midst of wolves: be ye therefore wise as serpents, and harmless as doves" (Matt. 10:16).

Once upon a time, in a certain land, there was this happy family that had just a son. His name was Uche. His parents, Nadi and Adafor, had him when they were sixty and forty-five respectively, after they had given up hope. His birth was God sent, and thus his name—Uche. He became very spoiled. Everybody knew he was rascally. If he went to play, he was there till night fell, and Adafor, his mother, had go get him. He cried for everything.

On this fateful day, Adafor prepared porridge, which was Uche's favorite meal, and kept it in the cupboard before leaving for the market. No one was at home when Nadi returned from the farm. Nadi ate the yam porridge in the cupboard that belonged to Uche. Nadi's portion was kept in another part of the room. As he was putting away the empty earthenware, Uche returned and dashed straight for his lunch. He nearly fell over Nadi as he rushed to get his food. Nadi quickly stepped aside and yelled at him,

"Can't you greet your elder first? I have told you that your mother has not trained you in the least of things, okay?"

Uche opened the first half of the cupboard and then the second, but there was no food. "Nadi, where is my porridge that Nene kept for me? Nadi, you ate my porridge." That was the custom in those days for children to call their mothers 'Nene' which meant, 'darling'.

Uche burst into tears and refused to be consoled. Nadi had to roast the rabbit that his trap had caught in the farm in order to appease Uche. He ate just a little portion, put the remainder in his back sac, and left to play with his friends. Two miles from the house, he met a farmer returning and got into conversation with him. The farmer was curious to know what Uche had in his bag. Uche showed him the leftover meal of rabbit meat, and the farmer snatched it from him and ate it. Uche burst into tears. He refused to be comforted. Passers-by urged the farmer to pay Uche for his meal. The farmer out of shame responded by giving him a beautiful beaded necklace. Uche was happy once more, and he scampered away.

No sooner had he travelled about five miles than he met an earthworm lying across the footpath. In those days, animals spoke and were understood by men. Uche asked the earthworm,

"What business do I have that you have to cross the entire footpath with your ugly length?"

Earthworm replied,

"All right, today you will know whether I am ugly or beautiful. Nobody crosses this path without paying a toll."

Uche replied,

"You are a liar. Get yourself off the road now before I kick you."

Earthworm said,

"We will see today who wins."

Everywhere that Uche turned, the earthworm was there. Uche was frustrated and didn't know what to do. They were in the middle of a thick forest. Uche was afraid of the wild animals. He longed to go home to his mother, but he couldn't. Suddenly he remembered his beaded necklace. He dipped his hand into his bag and threw the necklace at the massive worm. The earthworm jumped up and caught it before it landed on the path. It was gorgeous. The earthworm wound it round his neck and disappeared into the ground. Uche burst into tears and sang:

Oh earthworm, return my golden necklace;

The farmer gave me that necklace;

Because he ate my meat;

The meat that Nadi gave me;

Because he ate my porridge;

The porridge that Nene made;

Let the gods hear and judge.

Earthworm was never found to return what he had taken from man. But after the rain, earthworm crawled out of the hole, and behold every earthworm has a beaded necklace around its neck. That was Uche's necklace. Try and catch one and testify to this.

Let us pray: Powers assigned to steal from me, be arrested, in the name of Jesus.

Why Men Have Catarrh

"Out of the mouth of babes and sucklings hast thou ordained strength because of thine enemies, that thou mightest still the enemy and the avenger" (Ps. 8:2).

One day a woman went to fetch some firewood to cook for her family. She untied her son from her back and placed him on the wrapper on the footpath while she stepped into the bushes to cut some firewood. Every step took her farther into the bushes. There was a big millipede that was coming along the bush path as well. He was blind. Olu, the baby, saw him and started to cry for his mother to get him out of the way, but Mother was far into the bush.

Mommy, Mommy, Mommy, oooh, Mommy;

Come quickly and save your darling son, good Mommy

Oh return very soon, Mommy.

At this time, the millipede was fifty feet away. The baby sang again, but his mother was far gone into the bushes. Now the millipede was about ten yards away, but there was no mother. The baby just sat there and cried. The millipede crawled into the wrapper, and it went slowly into the baby's left nostril. Almost immediately, the mother returned with firewood. She didn't hear the baby's usual sound of welcome. She lifted him off the ground, and lo and behold, there was a big dead millipede blocking the nostril. She grabbed a tiny stick and tried to force it out. It was very difficult. Three quarters had gone into the brain. All the baby could do was to blow the nostril, and the result was thick, white-yellow frothy, and foul-smelling secretion. Some called it runny nose, others called it catarrh! Since then, man has continued to blow his nose or to clear his throat in severe cases of the flu or hay fever.

Let us Pray: Oh Lord, just as you delivered Daniel from the mouth of the lions, deliver me from the powers that are mightier than I, in Jesus' name.

Why Men Don't Have Tails

"Having then gifts differing according to the grace that is given to us, … according to the proportion of faith" (Rom. 12:6).

A long time ago in the country of Edumare, men and all the animals lived in houses. They shared everything in common. They went to the same market and bought and sold wares together. Ekun was the king.

News went around that Olodumare, the owner of the universe, wanted to distribute some gifts to all the animals and human beings alike in the next seven days. It was going to be a grand occasion that would take place in the next village square. Everyone was happy.

The day came, and all the animals and the humans set out for the journey. There were so many animals. They travelled very fast. The monkeys hopped from tree to tree. The birds flew. The dogs ran as fast as they could. The gift was to first come first served.

All the animals arrived on time and received the gift of long or short tails according to their destiny. The human was the last to get there because he was very slow. He couldn't run as fast as them. Olodumare dipped his hand into the bag, but there were no more tails. Olodumare was very sad because he had reserved the best of the tails for man, but now they were all gone, though not all the animals got tails, like the chimpanzees and Rottweiler. Olodumare promised to reserve wonderful tails for human after five millennia.

Let us pray: Remember me, oh God, according to your tender mercies. Let the portion of my blessings be delivered to me without labor, in Jesus' name.

Dike, the Great Wrestler

"Then I looked on all the works that my hands had wrought, and on the labor that I had labored to do and, behold, all was vanity and vexation of spirit, and there was no profit under the sun." (Ecclesiastes 1: 11).

A million years ago, all animals could speak. They communicated with themselves in languages known to them and some groups of men. They also lived in homes until these privileges were taken away from them. The humans were separated from the spirits by seven deserts, seven seas, seven forests, seven mountains, and seven rivers. The living did not have any serious interaction with the spirits, only when they chose.

In the land of the spirits, everything was special, and everything was there. There was special aircraft that took them anywhere. All they needed was to wear their special suits and they were there. Their markets were patronized by ghosts and diviners of special repute. Their foods were the best for human consumption. Their technologies were never outdated. They had special herbs that cured all ailments. They did not need to go to the hospitals. Their type of government was endless. There was no beginning. They had calm and peace. The living went there to seek power and wisdom. Anytime the living were around or visiting in the town, they knew the living were there. They had no seasons like the rain, sunshine, harvest, or *harmattan* as the living did. They only existed and assumed any form they pleased.

Dike the wrestler became subtle. He had conquered all the wrestlers in the towns far and near.

"I am the greatest wrestler," he boasted. "I have defeated all the champions in the land of the living. No man can challenge me."

"I will challenge you," a tiny voice said to him from behind.

"And I will beat you to your game."

A dialogue ensued between Dike and the voice, which belonged to a frog.

Dike said,

"Do you know who you are talking to? This is Dike, the great wrestler. The one who cannot be challenged. I have defeated seven times seventy-seven other wrestlers in all the villages combined. My wife, Omalicha, cooks and serves my meals with their skulls. Anyway, who am I talking to? I can hardly figure out where you are located."

Frog replied,

"I am the unbeatable froggie. The one that destroyed the northern armies. The one that caused commotion in the whole land of Egypt before the Pharaoh released the Israelites. I have been in existence before you, and I will prove to you that you are not my match!"

Dike said,

"I say shut up or I will stamp you out of existence."

Frog replied,

"Why don't you meet me in the next seven days at the market square in the land of the spirits and prove yourself the great wrestler that you think you are?"

With these words, Froggie hopped into the pond and disappeared. Dike was angry and humiliated. He could not sleep. He could not eat. His wife begged him to take it easy, but he would not be pacified. The chief of the village came to speak to him to be calm, but Dike was not to be calmed.

"This is an insult," he growled.

Omalicha reported the matter to Dike's mother. She was the backbone of Dike's success. She had three eyes. The third was invisible to the ordinary people. Froggie knew that she was about to die and Dike would have no more strength and that his back was about to be broken. Froggie was a ghost that had assumed animal form. Froggie had come for vengeance. Dike was sent for by his mother. He refused to respond. He passed by his mother's hut in search of his childhood friend Ogwu to accompany him to the wrestling game. He rudely shunned his mother, telling her that he had an assignment that needed an urgent attention and he would see her in the next seven days. Dike forgot one thing: that his strength was his mother.

The morning the two friends were to depart to the land of the spirits, news reached Dike that his mother had died. She had left a talisman, *inokpor,* to wear round his waist before going for any wrestling game. Dike had been blinded by rage. The only thing he thought about was how to beat his opponent to dust and use him for pepper soup.

The journey was tedious. There were many dangers to contend with. Wild animals chased them in the deep forests. They crossed the seven mountains, the seven rivers, seven oceans, and the seven deserts before arriving at the land of the dead. The market square was packed full. As soon as the two friends were sighted, a whistle blew to capture everyone's attention. The two friends refused every hospitality from the host. Dike wanted it to be done with so that he could return to bury his mother.

The game was getting very hot as the wrestlers continued to interlock in each other's arms. It was no longer Froggie the Wrestler but a human form with Froggie's voice. Dike was amazed, but the ugly voice taunted him, and he recalled their conversation. Suddenly Dike came to realize that he had challenged his destiny to a fight. It was his mother's spirit. She was a frog in the spirit. In the spirit world, there was no relation of any kind. Now it was too late to back out. All he would have done was to beg for his life on his knees, but anger was ready to make a fool of him. The crowd cheered, as they seemed to be entertained. Ogwu continued to blow his flute nonstop. He blew it till there was no more breath left in him. The wrestling had been going on for three days. All of a sudden, a scarecrow appeared in the sky and told Dike to run for dear life. Ogwu got the message, jumped into the ring, and pulled his friend away. They both took to their heels. All the ghosts chased these daring humans like a whirlwind. Ogwu's magical flute was the only hope.

Ogwu threw the flute into the air, and it turned to a big eagle. They flew across the seven deserts, seven seas, seven forests, seven mountains, and seven rivers. The ghosts were closing in as they entered into the human territory. Ogwu was the first to jump into the hut. As Dike was about to pull the door behind him, Froggie stretched his long finger, scratching the entire length of Dike's back from the neck to the waist, leaving a deep mark.

"This will teach you a lesson,"

he said as he returned from the pursuit. This was later replaced with a long spinal bone by God, running from the neck to the waist. Justin turned his back and showed them his back bone.

"Huh," they all sighed.

Let us pray: I command every spiritual pride in me and haughtiness of spirit to dissolve in the blood of Jesus, in Jesus' name.

Tears rolled down Ify's cheeks when she remembered Akabude in "A Dance in the Forest."

A Dance in the Forest

"He shall call upon me, and I will answer him;
I will be with him in trouble; I will deliver
him, and honour him" (Ps. 91:15).

Akabude was a very prosperous farmer. He farmed large acres of land. He had so many slaves who helped on the farm. He was also generous. All the villagers liked him. He gave to the poor and the needy. He was very scrupulous. He represented his village in inter-tribal conferences. He won the heart of many. But he was a sad man. Olie, his wife, has not been able to give him a son. He wanted a son so bad. Every day he wondered who would inherit his wealth when he died.

His friends and close associates taunted him and often asked him to start grooming a slave in his household who would inherit his riches. He was a confused man. He did not want to offend his wife, Olie. She had been betrothed to him at her birth. They had struggled and fought poverty together. How could he do this evil to his wife, the wife of his youth? The struggle continued and raged on within him.

At last, he decided to take a second wife with Olie's permission. He married a little girl chosen for him by Olie. She was called

Nkwo. She appeared very humble. She was beautiful. She would have been same age with Olie's child if she had a child. She seemed very charming and treated her mate with respect. As soon as she came into the household she started having babies. She had them yearly for ten years. Olie was very happy. The babies kept her busy. She was fulfilled. How she loved those children. While Nkwo was busy with house chores, Olie was busy teaching the children issues of life. They called her Mommy. Olie would wake up in the middle of the night to make sure they were sleeping well and that none of them had slept on the other by mistake. She would reposition the girls and have them properly covered. "A girl does not sleep with her legs thrown open," she would say as she repositioned them. They all loved her more than their biological mother. She nicknamed the last baby Mommy because she looked like Akabude's mother.

Akabude was still not happy. He secretly feared Nkwo, but he was not able to explain why. This continued for a long time. Once he confided his fears to Olie. Olie told him the love he had for her made him suspicious of Nkwo, and they would laugh it off. But not for long; Akabude died.

Three months after his funeral, Olie discovered that all was not well with her body. She jokingly asked Nkwo if it was possible for a woman to conceive after menopause. Nkwo went into the village and told everyone Olie was pregnant with a bastard. She told people who cared to listen that she had seen Olie several times with a stranger, whom she suspected was the father of the baby. Olie was actually fourteen weeks pregnant. She was two weeks pregnant before Akabude died. The wise women rallied around and supported her. They knew that Nkwo was evil, and no one paid attention to her.

Some days before Olie was due to deliver the baby, Nkwo was nowhere to be found. Olie was worried. This made the baby to come out earlier than scheduled. The labor was hard, and she died. A baby boy was born. He looked exactly like Akabude, and so he was called. For the purpose of our story, we will call him Bude. He grew into a handsome young man, a replica of his father. He was loved by all. He had favor because of his father's deeds.

Nkwo came forth in her full fury. Her craft was orchestrated to spoil. The first victim was Akabude, next was Olie, and now she was poised to get Bude. Bude was expelled and banished from the village after she had accused him of breaking into her room to rape her. By law, Bude would be allowed to appeal after seventy weeks for his innocence, but in the meantime, he had to go into exile. The villagers wept and bade him farewell. A certain old woman—an old friend to Olie—volunteered to accompany him because she was convinced Bude was innocent. She said,

"Is there any need for me to live, when I have no child and no relatives, and nobody will miss me?" she said sadly. So they embarked on the long journey.

They travelled in the wilderness for forty days and forty nights. They arrived at a country where there was no day and no night. The birds spoke and lived in homes. A big eagle welcomed them at the gate and gave them a home. They made Bude the king because he was different from them. Three days after his arrival, his companion and mother's friend died. Bude was sorrowful. He and the birds mourned her for weeks. He had told them she was his mother.

Life was hard for Bude in the birds' kingdom. They had just one kind of food. He got tired of the grains and launched into the forest for something new. As he wandered in search of familiar roots for food, he heard the sound of music from afar. Almost immediately, he dropped his bow and arrows, repositioned himself, and began dancing. He was so happy. The dancing continued for days, and then it suddenly stopped. He looked around, and there was an old lady smiling at him. "You will come here again tomorrow, and I will teach you the king's dance," she said to him. Bude didn't know what had come over him. All the birds had scattered all over the kingdom searching for him. He had been away for seven market weeks.

Bude continued to visit the old lady for dancing sessions, and this continued for a long time. On one particular day, the Old lady gave Bude an outfit and told him that he would need it someday in the future, and she was never seen again. Akabude was so sad, because he has lost two precious friends.

One day he heard one of the birds talking to another and saying that in a distant country, the king was holding a dance competition for all the males in the land. The winner would be given the princess for marriage. The sunbird, answered, "Do you know that our King has the uniform that was given to all the competitors?" Bude was stunned. What kind of uniform? Who gave it to him? He made inquiries and decided to attend the dancing competition wearing his gift outfit.

It was a long walk. He arrived on the last day of the ceremony. Beulah the beautiful had given up the hope of getting a good-dancing husband because none of them had satisfied her. As the chief umpire was about to blow the final whistle to declare the end of the contest, Bude jumped into the circle and screamed that somebody was omitted. The king asked the umpire to allow this dirty-looking man to have a chance. The music started. It was the same tune that Bude had listened to and often danced to in the forest. He knew the rhythm so well and the steps were in accordance.

The tune told the story of a wealthy man who had married a witch because his first wife could not bear him children and the witch had destroyed the entire household. It said that men should watch their steps. The song was in memory of Akabude, the rich man whose son was sent into exile. When the son's innocence was proved, the villagers went far and near to search for him but did not find him. The village minstrel had composed this song in the memory of the innocent child punished for the sin he did not commit. And the step-mother, Nkwo, had died a miserable death. But Bude did not understand the meaning of the rhythm.

He just danced with agility. The people cheered and cheered. They called him the lord of dance. The princess could no longer contain herself. She rose and entered the dancing arena. It was a sight to behold. She had schooled in the land of the spirits. She carried grace and splendor. She danced like the wind. Her other name was Dancing Queen. She danced toward Bude, went down on her knees, and bowed before him. The villagers jumped up in bewilderment. Princess Beulah had found a husband at last.

A wedding was planned. Bude married the princess and did not return to the land of the birds. He lived with his beloved wife in the palace, and they had beautiful children, who turned out to be the fairies and angels in the sky. "They bring you good tidings when you sleep," Justin added.

A jerk brought Ify back to reality. She had been daydreaming. She picked up her books and walked to the dormitory. Prep was over. It was time for her shower.

Let us pray: Holy Ghost fire, surround my goings and my comings, order my steps according to your tender mercies, and deliver me from my household's enemies, in Jesus' name.

Part Three

A New Dawn

The years had gone by so fast. Ify was in her final year. She had prepared very hard for the exam. She wanted to keep the promise she made to Justin. He had passed on the previous year after a brief illness. Ify found it difficult to believe that she was an orphan. Both of her parents had died uncelebrated. They refused to harvest their labor and the love they showered on their only daughter. It was hard for Ify to believe. She was alone in the world. What about her dreams of being the first university graduate in the family? Justin had promised her that he would live to see her through. But alas, death had taken a bitter toll on him. On the day she poured the sand over his coffin, she had told him that she would never fail him, and that if the dead could see, he would see her fulfilling her glorious destiny. Ify had returned to school with the determination to beat all odds.

It had not been easy. On that fateful morning when the news was broken to her in the principal's office, she had gone into a coma. She had always believed that Justin would never die—or at least not yet. He was still young. He had died after a brief illness. How brief? Justin had gone into a nearby pharmacy and purchased an expired medication that had reacted vigorously with his system and killed him. The hospitals were not adequately equipped to save lives; they were more like slaughter houses than anything else. Ify had lost a bosom friend who would be hard to replace. Life was becoming very challenging. Again she remembered those moonlight tales, and she was encouraged.

When school was out, she had to move to Uncle Gabriel's house in the village.

Sixty days had passed, and she was awaiting her final result. Ify had lost about twenty pounds since she took her exam. Her uncle urged her to eat, but she had little appetite. Her entire life depended on her high school results. She remembered again the story of the woman who had gone in search of firewood to prepare food for her family. When she got to the middle of the forest, she unstrapped her baby and laid him on a wrapper while she tied the pieces of wood with rope. A millipede crawled onto the wrapper and found its way into the child's nostril. The mother turned around to save her child, but it was too late. The creature had mingled with the baby's blood system and turned into mucous. "What does this teach us?" Justin would ask at the end of the story. Ify was more thrilled by the story than the message. She always looked forward to such nights because Justin was in a good mood. She got up from the recliner and blew her nose with a handkerchief.

She noticed a little red spot on the seat. Her flower had come. No wonder she had been nauseous for the past few days. She hid herself from her uncle for fear that he would ask too many questions. If her uncle found out, he would invite Theresa, her oldest auntie to start an investigation on her monthly periods. That was the last thing she wanted. Her exam results were her highest priority. She didn't want any distractions.

Ify quickly took a shower, cleaned up, and went back to the back porch. Then she heard Uncle Gabriel return. She met him at the door to greet him. He was smiling at her, and Ify wondered if he had hit a jackpot. It was a family of pool stakers. He had a box of malt drink, which Ify took from him and set on the table. He was followed closely by Auntie Theresa. Ify greeted her, and they both sat down. Ify's heart was pounding. She hoped none of those village boys had spoken to him about marriage. Ify had shunned all approaches by different suitors. She was not interested. Uncle Gabriel and Auntie Theresa had mounted pressure on her. Ify would not be convinced. They said, "It will not stop you from continuing with your education," or "Ify, you know, you are a girl. Very soon you will become too old and no man will come again," or "Ify, Mr. this and Mrs. that brought you some yams, and their son in America will be coming home, so they want you to visit him." Any time they talked like this, she remembered Justin. The last thing he would have done was force his daughter into marriage. Every night she would cry herself to sleep. If only Justin had stayed for her sake. When would she escape from these tortures?

She looked from Uncle Gabriel to Auntie Theresa. Ify was not ready for stories this evening. Uncle asked if she had dinner. "Yes, sir," she lied. He opened the first bottle of malt drink, gave it to Auntie Theresa, took the next one for himself, and gave the third to Ify. The silence was broken. He dipped hand into his sack and brought out an opened brown envelope. Ify held her chest.

Oh Lord, what is it, this time? she thought.

Her heart was racing like wild fire. She started getting ready for a defense. But she was very wrong. That was not the case. It was the contrary. Uncle Gabriel continued to smile. He had stumbled on good news. He took a glass and poured out some of the drink as libation on the floor with these words:

"Justin, today your daughter has vindicated you. You labored to see this day, but you were denied."

Ify went closely and discovered that it was a letter stating she had passed her general certificate in education in grade one. She screamed and held on to Uncle Gabriel. Auntie Theresa hugged her. There was another envelope that stated she had been offered admission to the University of Lagos. She was to study French language and education.

There was no time to prepare. The admission had come very late. School would resume in two weeks. All the education courses were paid for by the federal government. Ify needed some money to purchase a few things before going. Uncle Gabriel, Auntie Theresa, and Victoria, the junior auntie put their heads together, borrowed money from the community safe, and gladly sent her to school. Ify was very glad and promised them to always remember their generosity to her. She remembered her father again, and she wept. Her father had been her backbone in all things.

The University of Lagos was one of the oldest colleges in the country. She was in Amina Hall. There were too many wild parties held in the honor of the freshers. Ify was not cut out for such things, so she did not attend. The Christian fellowship was what attracted her attention, and she honored their invitation. She felt very much at home with this group of individuals. She loved their outings, and they taught her how to pray. She was glad she was in their midst. It was hard to live on the allowance, but she was able to cope. In her second year, she met a young man from her village named Charlie. They began to see each other frequently, and news reached Uncle Gabriel and Auntie Theresa that she had met a suitor at last.

Ify and Charlie

He was called Charlie. He was of average height, light complexioned, and a former school footballer. He was soft spoken, very cautious, and chose his words carefully. A woman would rightly describe him as a fine gentleman with good prospects. He was not given to wealth but had a promising career. He shared a flat with another old school mate, Sam. His old father was a retired World War II veteran who had inherited a three-room brick home from his father, a renowned and ebullient farmer. Charlie's father's name was Yke. He had two wives, Helen and Helena. Helen was Charlie's mother, the first wife. Helena, the second wife, was a couple of years, or less, older than Charlie.

Life in a polygamous setting was stiff and bedeviled with all manner of evil, rivalry, jealousy, gossip, fighting, and competition. There was nothing good to write about it. Charlie recalled that some nights they would be woken by loud noise from fights between Yke and Helen in their one-room apartment. Yke would be transferred from one army unit to another, so Charlie and his siblings lived in nearly all the major towns in the country. His education had always been interrupted. He had to start over at every new location. Helen had become weary and therefore refused to accompany him in the last posting, so Yke eventually invited

Helena into the household as a second wife. Helen had chosen to stay in the village to raise the children so they could have a proper education, which never went well with Yke. His threat became reality and birthed polygamy. Helen got ready for a battle and vowed to make life miserable for Yke. When he finally retired from active service in the army, Yke collected his entitlements and benefits and lavished them on his nuptial ties with Helena. Helen felt cheated, and the rift between them deepened. The only comfort was in her sons. Her first daughter had been given in marriage to a farmer whose wife had just passed on.

Helen was very hardworking, black, and beautiful. Many men desired to have her as a wife. She took up the challenge and raised her sons. Yke was never there for the boys. She became the man of the house. Yke was occupied with baby making with Helena. They had eleven children before he died. Helena had double births thrice, and all the children lived. At this time, Charlie was ready for secondary school, but Yke was unable to sponsor him. Helen's younger brother came to the rescue. He paid for a year's education at a nearby vocational school. Charlie's grandfather had to intervene before Yke took over the sponsorship of his education.

Charlie would recall with tears that on one occasion, he nearly lost his life in a fatal accident that claimed many lives when he went to search for his father to pay his school fee. Helen frequented all the village markets, buying and selling cassava flour, plantains, cocoa, palm nuts, kola nuts, peanuts, and whatever she could to bring in money. She was not going to be a pushover and would not be challenged in the household. Like a peacock, her presence and authority was not going to be overshadowed. She was to be reckoned with. She was fearless. Helena cowered at her presence.

Sooner than expected, news spread all over the town that that Ify, the daughter of Justin, was getting married. The first step was for both families to get to know each other. Each family investigated about each other's family records and histories. They had to find out if those who wished to marry were destined for one another. They had to find out if there were family records of special illnesses that might affect their future children. They had to find out if there was history of premature deaths, epilepsy, miscarriages, robbery, mental disorders, or whatever was an abomination to their culture. More importantly, the man's family had to know if the woman had any bad luck attached to her destiny, like barrenness or albinism in the family. Another major inquiry was whether the woman had been circumcised. The tradition would never permit a man from this culture to marry a woman who was not circumcised. They believed that the woman would not be able to give birth to children and that she would end up as prostitute in the man's home. That was not going to be the issue because Ify had been circumcised.

When a girl was born into any family, she would be circumcised by the oldest woman after eight days. The baby's mother would get two white roosters, native chalk, a sharp knife or razor blade, and a white piece of cloth. No ceremony was held without the breaking of *kolanuts*. The ancestors had to be appeased and permission had to be sought for the successful operation of the circumcision. Tutu, the circumciser, was renowned. She had done it for all the girls in Ify's family. People who were not related to her also contracted her for this event.

When Tutu was needed to circumcise Ify, she was becoming too old and had to get the help of her eldest daughter, Ada. Ada would hold the baby firmly, with one hand clamping down the arms and another holding one of the legs, while Old Tutu groped with her fingers, searching for the right place to chop off.

Sometimes the baby's father would assist by pointing a flashlight in between the legs for better vision. Tutu would pull the foreskin very tight and then aim at the base. The white cloth would be used to wrap the bleeding wound. When the bleeding slowed down, alligator pepper would be sprinkled over the wound or iodine might be applied. After eight market days, the wound would be healed. The infant would never have to know the pain because she was still very small.

Ify was a complete woman. She had gone through this ordeal as an infant from what Gracie had told her. When these studies were concluded, a date was fixed for an informal introduction before the traditional and then church wedding.

Ify's Traditional Wedding

The ceremony was to take place in the evening. There was a canopy in front of Uncle Gabriel's big compound. Uncle had earlier called a family meeting and told everyone that certain in-laws would be visiting. It was going to be the first visit from the bridegroom's family. Thirty minutes before their arrival, Uncle Gabriel and the rest of the family were seated, saying traditional prayers before the family altar. The in-laws had arrived in a white mini-bus. Charlie was missing from the group. Yke was there, as well as some elders and Helen. They set before their hosts three kegs of palm wine, three cartons of beer, three bottles of brandy, and some kolanuts. Uncle Gabriel and his family members rose to their feet as the guests entered. There were exchanges of greetings and pleasantries before they finally settled into their seats. The oldest in Justin's family welcomed the guests again before proceeding to break the kolanuts. He offered prayers to his ancestors, invoking their spirits to guide and attend the ceremony, at the end of which everybody responded, "Amen!" He invoked Justin's spirit to be in attendance because the ceremony was a manifestation of his hard labor.

The next to take the floor was an elder from Yke's family who rose to thank their host for opening his doors to them. He said,

"Our ancestors often said, when you see a frog hopping in the day time, you surely know there is something pursuing it. We have known this family for a long time, and the will of our ancestors has brought us here this evening. We have an illustrious son in the city very far from here, and he has sent us here. Our son told us that there is a beautiful girl in this compound who can only bring happiness into his life, one who he will not be able to resist. Her name is Ify. This is the great lady who has brought us here."

The whole crowd applauded him as he took his seat. There was a pause as Uncle Gabriel deliberated the discussion with the rest of the family. Then the guests were served some food. Ify had decided to entertain her guests with a special delicacy. They were to be served fried plantain and fish stew. That was the latest trend in the town. All the recent celebrations were not complete without this menu. The day before, Uncle's wife had gone to the market and purchased ripe plantains. She also enlisted some women and neighbors to assist in the cooking.

When all had eaten and drunk some wine, the spokesman from Justin's family stood and welcomed them again and announced that the mother of the house had been sent to find out who among their daughters was worthy of this noble visit. That was the custom, even if the bride was there. After some time, she would return to give the message to the elder that the daughter had gone to the market and would be notified immediately. The spokesman would then inform the guests that they had come to the right house and that their doors were opened at their command. This was a positive indication that the bridegroom was welcomed to the family and that he should proceed to the next stage of the tradition. That was the traditional introduction or "knocking at the door" in which the dowry will be paid. A date would be agreed as to when this would take place.

Payment of dowry varied among families and cultures. Prior to that day, a list would have been given to the family of the bridegroom in readiness for all that was requested by the family of the woman. Every male child in the house of the wife's family would share from the bride price.

The women would share bags of salt, onions, and rice. Ify had to travel to the village for this ceremony in the company of her friends. Aunty Christy, Uncle Gabriel's wife, had purchased all the items Ify would need to start a new home. Most of the traditional wares have been replaced by modern machines, like pounding and the blender instead of the wooden mortar and the grinding stone. There were cooking pots and clothing for her new baby.

The day of the dowry was very colorful. There was lots of food and drinks and music everywhere. There were canopies and people dressed in their best attire. Photographers positioned themselves and took snapshots of the event. Ify was dressed in traditional regalia. She had her hair decorated with coral beads. Charlie had the men's long shirt and wrapper and a cap on the head. The men sat away from the women. The family spokesman would go through the entire list to make sure nothing was omitted. After this, they would settle down to eat. On the other side, Aunty

Christy would receive Ify's mother's share of the dowry from the mother of the groom and then transfer it to Ify in the presence of the women.

Literally two prices were being paid: one for the father and the other for mother of the woman. That is the tradition. If this was not correctly applied, Ify's in-laws would look down on her as a cheap woman. There were other parts of the culture that would equate the dowry to the amount spent on the university education of the woman. In Ify's case, only a token to symbolize that their daughter was not a woman of easy virtue was requested. Justin had always made it clear he would never behave like the other parents who charged a large amount because their daughter had attended the university. Gracie had ever hoped for the best for her only daughter, and her main concern was for Ify to have a happy home. She was not for sale.

Another aspect of the tradition was the dance of the new couple. After the payment of the dowry, it was time for the couple to open the dance floor. Ify was beautiful and an indisputable great dancer. Dressed in traditional short wrapper around her waist and another wrapper over her breasts, she stepped into the dancing floor, followed closely by her maids of honor, also known as her unmarried friends. This was going to be the last dance or the last time she would be seen in public with spinsters. Her figure eight was alluring. She had hot, straight legs as she led the group toward her future husband. She knelt down in obeisance while her husband rose and placed the big fan on her back as a gesture of approval.

The local music was powerful. Ify swung around in a swift twist. She threw up her arms, shook her waist, and turned to the left, bending double as she moved toward the floor. The next minute she was in her full height, wriggling her entire body. It was a fire dance. The crowd applauded. Uncle Gabriel was happy that his brother's effort had not been in vain. Regardless of the odds, the family had produced its first university graduate. It was worth the celebration. The in-laws nodded their heads in approval that Ify was a real woman in all respect. Then it was her friends' turn. All the young men searching for brides joined in the dance. This continued the whole night.

Two weeks or less later, there would be the white or court wedding. The service would take close to two hours. Next was the reception in another part of the town. Ify and Charlie believed that was a one-time ceremony in a couple's life. They loved every moment of it. Ify wished that both her parents could have witnessed these occasions. All the sections were started with the remembrance of the departed souls. Ify burst into tears as soon as Justin and Gracie's names were mentioned.

The final stage was the escort to the husband's home. It always took place in the night. The father and mother of the woman would pray and bless their daughter, that she would prosper in this journey she was undertaking, that she would be mother of twins and a comfort to her husband. All the unmarried friends and relations, amidst tears, hugging, and dancing, would bid her farewell. Ify would no more be found in the company of spinsters; she had a new role. She had joined the "wrapper ladies"—no more skirts and blouses. She would wear wrappers and blouses from then on. Ify's mother-in-law received her at the door. She washed Ify's feet, wiped them clean, and welcomed her into her new home.

The following day was a Sunday. Both families attended the church's thanksgiving service in appreciation for God's mercies. After this, the young couple was on its own. Ify had assumed a new role as wife and mother-to-be—the roles she would play for the rest of her life.

Life with Charlie

Charlie did not resemble his mother. He was not a hustler. He worked for a big food industry where he rose to the position of top management by God's grace. He discharged his duties to the best of his knowledge and retired after twenty five years of meritorious service as an electrical engineer. They both had four wonderful children, a girl and three boys. Ogor, his oldest son has rightly described him as, "a worthy civil servant without scruples." He and Ify had great challenges as a couple at the beginning. The family depended on meager salaries that barely sustained them. Ify had to search for other means to improvise in order for the kids' school fees to be paid. She opened a little grocery store, where she spent most of her evenings after work. She had taken a job as a school teacher, but the income was nothing to write home about. The school fees for one of the kids was exactly her monthly salary. The best she could do was to make a payment plan with the school authority so that at the end of the session, all the fees would be paid. Life was very rough. On some evenings, Charlie would use their Peugeot station wagon as taxi cab to make ends meet. She never lost hope. She believed that this would end someday, and it actually did.

A few years later, Charlie was able to buy Ify a little car. She was able to take the kids to school and get herself to her own job. Things were beginning to take a new turn. She was able to get better clothing for the entire family and attend mid-week church services with the kids. God has answered her prayers, and she became more devoted than ever. On Saturdays, she would take the kids to the local church. They would sweep and mop the entire church and clean the toilets for no charge. She loved the assignment. The kids went to fetch the water from the well while she mopped the floors. She also worked in the children's department, where she taught as a Sunday school teacher. She was able to keep a close watch over her kids.

God was faithful to his promises. When the time came for the local pastor to nominate a member to attend a course in children's education ministry sponsored by the regional headquarters, Ify was chosen because of her dedication. She loved working with the kids. She believed that every child was talented in a particular field. In secular education, as a school teacher, she never believed in failing a child. According to her, failure was lack of effective communication with the child because proper teaching had not taken place. She loved her job, though she was poorly paid. She had time to go over her kids' homework do corrections with them. Charlie contributed by being a good father. His presence enforced the house laws and order. He was called Papa Cee. Any kid who failed to wash the dishes, sweep the house, or clean the kitchen would receive a whipping. There was no bullying or fighting at school or in the house. Everyone had to go to bed at eight o'clock promptly after prayers. Ify taught her children to love God.

On one fateful day, Ify went to the beauty shop to have her hair done when one of their neighbors rushed in to inform her that Ogor, then seven years old, had fallen and sustained a serious injury. She left almost immediately and on getting home, Ify discovered that Ogor had climbed the fence, missed a step, and fallen over one of the fence spikes, which narrowly missed the last rib at the right side. There was so much blood by the time she arrived at the hospital with him. He got many stitches, and after that, Ify always kept a close watch on him.

Another time, Ogor climbed the pillar from the second floor to the ground floor when he and his sister were locked up in their apartment. Ify had just returned from school, was exhausted, and went to sleep on the couch in the parlor. As usual, Ogor wanted to play with his mates downstairs, but the doors were locked. The only way was to climb the pillar on the patio and get downstairs. Passers-by saw him and had to extend their hands to catch him as he was falling. He was a gifted climber.

He went on to graduate from the university at twenty-one with a degree in mechanical engineering. Ify told her friends that Ogor had promised to buy her and Charlie an airplane. She has never forgotten, and she still believes. Ogor had other siblings, an older sister and two younger brothers, all graduates of universities. The sister got married to a businessman immediately after graduating from the university. Ify had always emphasized that her children should marry people from good Christian homes. According to her, a marriage built on God's principles endured hard times.

Ify's life as a married woman was not particularly rosy, but it was better than the misery Gracie had endured with Justin. Ify was very tolerant and patient. Many issues confronting both her and Charlie were resolved amicably between them without a third party. Definitely no third party had ever been involved in their disputes, no matter how heated the argument become. Many issues had to be debated, but she never lost her good sense as to challenge the authority of the man. Ify recalled a special case that would have led to separation, but wisdom prevailed. The only grounds that could lead to divorce in a marriage was when the woman was unfaithful.

A real African woman at that time had to realize that she was born into a culture of multiple wives to one man. The black man was seen as polygamous and instinctively endowed with promiscuity. It was an abomination for the woman to live such lifestyle. A woman taken in adultery would lose all entitlements and benefits from her husband and respect from her family members. She became an outcast in the society. She would bring a curse from almighty God. No one would ask for the hands of her daughters in marriage for fear of pollution. Her sons would never earn the respect of the people in the society. She would become a taboo. Today that no longer matters. The society is in conflict with itself concerning this issue.

Disagreeing to Agree

Ify approached Charlie as he was resting in bed. She knew this was a perfect time. It was Friday night, so he had no job the next day. She sat on the chair beside the bed and poured out her soul. She started by telling him what had taken place between her and their eldest son concerning an issue Charlie had reported to him. It has been a telephone conversation. The voice at the end of the telephone was angry and bitter. The story was one sided. Charlie had a convincing way of winning issues. He was usually cautious. Ify had learned his style over the years. To floor him, Ify had to be prepared, or she would end up looking stupid, even when she was not at fault. Not again. Ify was ready this time. She had her facts memorized and rehearsed several times. She would have victory.

She opened the discussion with a greeting, *"Uwaoma,"* which literarily means, "Good evening, elder." The response was, "Same to you." She started by introducing the subject of the accusation, which was, according to him, an abomination in their tradition. She talked about what Ogor had expressed in their conversation, and then she rattled on. She reminded him about a similar complaint from a family member—that she was not living up to her responsibilities as a wife. Her response then was that it took two to make a union succeed, for it was written in the Bible that two cannot walk together unless they were in agreement. For this reason, the man would leave his father and mother and be joined to his wife, and the two would become one. She explained that this was the oldest institution God had created and laid down. Physically it was impossible for two objects to become one, but this was a spiritual union whose mathematics defied the law of nature, even physics. A marriage that was not built in the Spirit would be in crisis. Sexual gratification and satisfaction are just minute aspects to fulfilling a happy union. Sex is not love; it is one ingredient out of many. But love takes the lion's share. Famous poets, great writers, and scholars have tried to describe love through writing and imagery, but none has described it as accurately as the picture given by Paul, the Pharisee turned apostle, as recorded in the Holy Bible.

> Love is patient, love is kind. It does not envy. It does not boast, it is not proud. It is not rude, it is not self-seeking. It is not easily angered, it keeps no record of wrongs. Love does not delight in evil but rejoices with the truth. It always protects, always trusts, always hopes, always perseveres. Love never fails.(1Cor.13:4-8 NIV)

Is this a perfect kind of love she had invested in with all her years? She had loved blindly.

She lost both parents when she needed them. The only available choice was Charlie. Had Charlie really loved her as he confessed? She had often asked herself. In the Western world, the love system is identical to that laid by the Apostle Paul, God's own standard. The African man will never understand what it takes to love. Ify remembered the story Justin narrated about the lover boy who never stopped confessing, "Abigail is the only sugar in my cup of tea." She also recalled the farmer who married the Londoner. He called a family meeting to report to the wife's mother that he received the biggest shock of his life when his wife called him *darling* in the presence of the other farmers. It was not their custom. People thought that he had been charmed by his wife. That was an African man caught in the web of modern ideology.

Black men believe in exercising authority and power over their wives. As far as they are concerned, their wives are just like another piece of furniture, to be used and discarded or to be placed in a quiet place and not exposed. If a black man has riches, then every single penny would be used to purchase a wife. She had no right or mind of her own anymore. Ify was caught between education and tradition.

Ify's mother tolerated insults from her father because she was not educated. Ify told herself that no man was going to treat her like that. After three years, Justin and Gracie's marriage was over. Gracie was not properly educated, and Justin wanted a wife who spoke and understood English language, or that was his excuse. Gracie left with their only daughter and stayed with Ezuno. All pleas for Justin to return to his wife fell on deaf ears. Later they both remarried and went their different ways.

Gracie's second husband was no better than the first. He was very possessive and never gave her freedom in life. He was bedeviled with jealousy and distrust. He went after other men's wives and thought that same was happening with his wife. Justin was a certified woman batterer. The later husband lavished his energy on old spinsters and was an expert in giving them babies. Gracie mentioned to Ify that his was a special gift. He was the transit for women looking for babies. He went out in the thickness of the night with a hand torch and returned in the early hours of the morning. Gracie never dared to challenge him. In the end, Gracie contracted a sexually transmitted disease—cancer of the cervix—which eventually killed her. They had been married for nearly twenty years.

Ify found herself again interlocked between vengeance and morality. Her newfound culture in Christianity had a deep hold on her. Confessions and testimonies that she heard from reliable sources brought her to the conclusion that some humans were possessed by devils. Her mother had been a victim at the hands of cruelty. She continued to wonder why any husband would want to betray a trust and chose misery. She knew Justin was good father in all ways but a horrible husband. That fact was hard on her. Would she want to avenge and become reckless because of the bad portion that her mother had received?

Ify was a traditional homemaker. She never believed in equality with her husband. Many times she told her friends that it was unbiblical especially for a woman to strive for equality with the husband in the home. They both had different functions and roles. She was an advocate of one-man, one-wife and total submission to husband's authority. Husbands were created to supply the needs of the family. The man would go to the farm at dawn and return in the evening. She would be at home to meet his needs. An additional for the role for the woman as a homemaker was to be a booster.

The godly husband who sees ahead of time is a provider and protector of his family. Ify's desire was for a husband who shared the same faith as her. She would have loved a husband who shouted and sang alleluia with her in the front pew every Sunday—a husband who would go out all morning and return into her waiting arms. She never asked for one whose eyes roamed to and fro at whatever was in a skirt! She didn't want to play second fiddle in the heart of any man.

Another aspect Ify had to contend with was intrusion of mother-in-law. Some mothers refused to let go. An interesting point here is that these types of mothers never allow anyone to interfere in their own marriages. They were in absolute control and lorded over their husbands. Many marriages have collapsed because of the overpowering evil nature of these mothers over their sons or daughters. The victims allow their mothers to control their lives at will.

Ify made her dislike of husbands who remained in the grasp of their mothers clear to anyone who would listen. She remembered the story of the groom whose mother taught him how to lose his virginity. Ify wanted a real man! God made her a woman. God endowed her with virtues. She was proud to be a woman.

She recalled the story of her childhood friend, Janet, whose husband told the pastor of the church that he had decided to have an extramarital affairs because Janet would not oblige his sexual desires as requested. Her mother-in-law had called her wedding a "caricature" or a "wedding behind the pulpit." Janet and John had quietly gone to the marriage registry in the next town while her mother-in-law was babysitting for them without her knowledge. All they had for witnesses were John's brother, who stood for John, and Willy, John's cousin, who stood for Janet. It was a pastor's style of wedding—that is, only very close family members were in attendance. Janet had borrowed her outfit from a close friend, but that didn't mean anything to her. John had told her that his marriage was nobody's business, not even his mother's.

John's mother had never forgiven them. She had wanted a big wedding for her only successful son. John was very prudent.

He hated flamboyance. But now Janet knew better. Had it really made any difference? Her mother-in-law had forever taunted her for this. Though their marriage had endured stormy weather, if she was given another opportunity, she would sing a different tune. "My marriage would be wedding of the century," she said. Ify had reminded her that the photos taken did not tell sad stories. Her mother-in-law had said worse things about them that really didn't mean anything, but as time passed, Janet discovered that they were very derogatory. The statements had portrayed her and her family as cheap. According to Janet, if John had spent his money for a wedding for her as other men did for their wives, he would have had more value for her. John's brother had mentioned that Janet tricked John into marrying her because Janet was pregnant.

At the end of Ify's ranting, Ify wanted to know some answers to some pertinent questions that had troubled her. She had some issues she could not disclose to her closest friend. She didn't want stories to be let out of the bag, so she had chosen silence. Charlie would always choose a club instead of church. He would rather go late and arrive at benediction but would be the first in a social gathering. He declined all marriage counseling. It was an intercourse of troubled thoughts, and a lot of it had to do with his promiscuity.

All the while, Charlie was lying on his back, listening. He faced Ify and said, "You have made yourself look like an angel and me the devil. You lock your room because I should not enter. Why won't I go to church? I believe in God. Do I have to go to church to prove it? You were on vacation and did not bother to attend my uncle's funeral. You could have looked for money and gone. Are you saying there would have been no one to loan you some money? You cannot progress unless you recognize I am the man of the house. You engage me in a tug of war. No, you can't move forward till you know that I am a man." He snapped his fingers. "Let's go on with the battle. But let me assure you, I am going to make it with or without you. Remember, whatever the decision made, some people will be adversely affected. You treated my mother shabbily. You insulted my mother. You say you want to succeed …"

For close to an hour, it was Ify's turn to listen, and she did with rapt attention. At the end she demanded clarifications here and there. The issue of his mother had been a long-standing matter that demanded acute wisdom. His mother would not let go. There was a secret tussle between her and Ify. Helen wanted total control over Charlie, and she manipulated him with impunity. Ify reminded him that if Lucifer had seen that Jesus was going to have a better glory, he would not have nailed Jesus to the cross. And as sure as heaven was real, no power was capable of stopping her from succeeding in all her endeavors. Ify had discerned that Charlie had a vendetta because of his mother.

Both of them concluded that a marriage was between the man and wife. Any third-party involvement was unacceptable and must never be entertained. The issue was not to be his mother but them!

Ify's In-Laws

Ify did not get along with her in-laws. The mother-in-law wanted it her way in their home, which did not go well with Ify. Ify had always wondered why some of her mother-in-law's outbursts were sometimes offensive. Ify had always admired her courage in raising her children single-handedly and enduring the many insults from a polygamous home. Perhaps people were right when they said how much she had labored for her sons, and no other woman or sons' wives would have it easy with her. Charles's mother had vowed to get her revenge because of the pains she went through with her husband's second wife.

After Charles's father married the second woman, Helena, Charles's mother became a reproach. Charles's father had used all his pension and benefits to pay for the dowry of his new wife, Helena. She was two years older than Charles. Yke, Charles's father, refused to listen to reasoning that it was only rich men who invested in wives and not poor men like him. He was an ordinary soldier with no rank in the civil army that he had retired from. Neither was he a prosperous farmer. Yet he went ahead and got married to a second woman. Helen did not take it lightly and vowed to get revenge and make life miserable for him. Yke and Helena would team up and beat Helen mercilessly, leaving her with broken teeth and sometimes with a broken jaw and swollen face.

Helen was undaunted. She fought like lioness. She challenged Yke in secret and in broad daylight. She contended with Helena in all places, including high altars. She was not their match, and she beat them at their games. She had the support of Yke's father and the villagers. The senior brother was no pushover. He rose and fought Yke in secret and openly. Yke was a man of tradition, and he managed to prevail. Their family set up was in cold wars. They battled over everything, and most of it was supremacy. Helen became the goddess-mother of the home.

Her sons could not question her audacity. It was a fight to the finish. She extended her tentacles in her trade and won the hearts of men in the village. Black and beautiful, her dance steps and sonorous voice were charming. She was everywhere. People wanted to be identified with her. Sometimes she would be gone for days, trading from one town market to another. She gave trouble to those that wanted it, and for those who loved peace, she gave it. She may have lost her position in the heart of her husband, but she did not lose among her friends and other groups in the village. She loved the tradition of her forefathers, of which her senior brother was the custodian. Helen built a three-bedroom bungalow to occupy a space that would have been inherited by another member of the family. She would have rather died than to see someone else occupying the piece of land. According to her, it belonged to Charlie. Yke had given out other portions of the property for a keg of palm wine and few pennies. Helen had often commented that since Yke married his second wife, he had lost all reasoning.

Yke was an unassuming character. He was very easygoing.

Both women did not listen to him. He couldn't manage their outbursts. They were volatile when they decided to erupt. They outwitted him in the village tribunals. He would end up paying fines for an offense he did not commit. The women were sworn secret enemies. More than once, he had threatened to commit suicide. He would carry his double-barreled gun to shoot himself. The entire village would surround him, trying to get it from his grip. Only his pension gave him a little joy, but it was short lived. When he returned from receiving his pay, Helena was at the door to snatch the money from him. Helen was never given her part of the pension as demanded by the tradition of the land.

Yke's life revolved around these two women. He had no control over his household. Old age was fast approaching. Agility had left him. He had succumbed to the mercies of these powerful women. Helen only existed for her children. She had often made it clear that it was Charlie who made her remain in the family or she would have returned to her father's house.

She was richly dressed and bought expensive wrappers and blouses. They made her the mother of the day in all occasions. She rubbed shoulders with the rich in the town. She spoke Pidgin English when it was necessary. Ify had recalled several occasions she had told her in Pidgin, "Na only English that you can speak pass me, you hear, I big pass you." None of her children were able to surpass her in natural strength and audacity.

Helen chose to be the general overseer of her sons' homes. Ify vehemently refused this. Ify resisted her. It didn't go well with both ladies. Helen manipulated in whatever means available to her to control, or so it seemed, but she was forcefully held back. Charlie yielded. Helen did not care whose toes she stepped on to have her way, but Ify continued to resist. Charlie dared to challenge her. She controlled by proximity and remotely. Ify admired her mother-in-law but feared her secretly.

Helen was always welcomed in Ify and Charles's home. When Ify went to work, Helen would take care of the house and did the chores. They got on well in the beginning until an evil rivalry sneaked in between them. It was youthfulness versus ageing. Helen forgot the age difference. They were not to be compared. They played different roles in Charlie's life.

The feud between the two women continued for a long time. It became warfare. Ify had no one to report to. She thought the problem would be compounded. Justin had three wives before he died, his brother, Uncle Gabriel, had uncountable wives, and her aunties had more than two husbands. Nobody was qualified to give counsel that would sustain her marriage. Her problem was Helen. Gracie had told Ify to keep on with prayer and never trust anyone for help, and she did. Gracie had spoken to her about the golden rule, which was silence. "Telling people your problem is like a broadcast," she had warned Ify. Neither did she play into the hands of miserable comforter friends.

Helen's youngest son was another source of trouble. Ify described him as one whose sole ambition was to be a parasite on the elder brother. He flouted Charlie's orders with impunity. He had no respect for Ify. Once he had attempted to assault her. He had refused to acknowledge Ify as Charlie's wife. Helen had willed him to Charlie as an inheritance. Charlie's biological children were to be placed second after Mike. This fact became more glaring as days went by. Helen was ready to destroy whatever would stand as obstacle against her hidden agenda. Many times Ify had confronted Charlie with this, but he had denied it.

When Yke died, Charlie inherited an old, leaking mud house with three bedrooms and one kitchen, Helena, her eleven children, his mother, and an acre of patched farm land. The seven books of Moses were still missing. Yke wanted his son to learn about the mysteries contained in that book. He was glad he was going to pass the children on to Charlie because, according to him, there would be many suitors asking for the hands of the girls for marriage. Charlie would be there to receive the father's dowry from them all.

Yke was a nice old man. He was a people person. Uncle Gabriel had once mentioned that he had consented to the marriage with the family because of Yke. Yke loved Ify. When he visited them in the city, he would tell stories of World Wars II and II. He told how his garrison commander had allowed him to visit Jerusalem and how he had fought Adolf Hitler in Germany. Ify was always thrilled by those stories. Yke mentioned the day he pissed in his pants when he saw a bearded Israeli woman soldier in Jerusalem. He had never seen a woman with a beard. Yke would go to the forest to hunt for venison to entertain Ify. He always returned with rabbits and little yams. He was a good man.

Part Four

Ify Goes to America

Ify remembered a day when she had visited the village with Justin. They came to the marketplace, and there was a man in weird clothing dancing around a casket. He was surrounded by a large crowd. He was in a frenzy as he chanted, "Come and see the American wonder. Come and see the American wonder."

He would jump very high into the air with a cutlass, twisting his entire body like an Indian rubber ball, and down again he went. The show was endless. Sometimes he would ask his partner to stab him several times in the chest, only to find him in another spot in the audience. Justin said he was a magician. Ify had never liked magicians. They were weird and liars. The shows were incredible.

Now Ify had an opportunity to go to the America she had often heard about. Ify had visited a friend who had recently returned from America. Patricia had narrated all she saw in America. She had stayed in New York and visited so many places. She travelled to Dallas in Texas and Hollywood in Los Angeles and visited the casinos in Las Vegas, Six Flags of Dallas, and New Orleans in Louisiana. Ify listened with amazement and attention. How she had longed to visit these beautiful places. The electric train, the double-decker passenger buses, and the skyscrapers were astonishing and sounded like fairy tales. To crown her story, Patricia said there was never electric power failure. Light shone all the time, day and night.

"You mean there are no blackouts in America?" Ify asked.

Patricia said, "Even their roads are all tarred, and there is concrete everywhere. You can't see ordinary ground. Hon, you should see the way the traffic moves—it is just like soldier ants in a single file. Their police patrol in vehicles."

Ify's peace was shattered. All night she dreamt of going to America. The next day, she went back to Patricia's house for more information. Patricia had found willing ears, and she was merciless in her descriptions. "My brother and I went to Chicken Burger. We ate all we could for only one dollar. Everywhere there was fast food … and if you could see how big these people are."

"What do you mean? Are they bigger than us here?" Ify asked.

"Aahh, they are very big. Ooh, people are sick of food there. Do you remember how the garden of Eden was in the Bible? My friend, that is America for you. There were taxis everywhere," she concluded.

The stories were endless. Ify was thrilled and overwhelmed by each narration. That was exactly the image of the lost paradise. She finally asked Patricia for information about procuring a visa to the United States of America.

Her mind was made up to visit this great country of the Earth. She was going to apply as soon as the children were on vacation. Ify went ahead and requested her older cousin, who lived in America, for a letter of invitation and the supporting travelling documents. Her cousin obliged but said that a third party was not allowed to touch any copy of the individual citizen's certificate. The only remedy would be for one to appear in person with the interviewee on that day at the embassy. Ify trusted her cousin. After all, he'd been there long enough to know the rules and regulations. The day of the interview drew close, and Ify became very uncomfortable about stories of how many individuals had been denied entry into the United States.

The day she was scheduled for the interview came, but her big cousin was nowhere to be found. She encouraged herself in God and left amidst prayer and fasting. God gave her favor before the interviewer. She was given two years with multiple entries. To crown the victory, her husband, Charlie, wrote a check to cover the flight ticket. She was to travel with a first-class ticket. The transit visa was issued, and Ify proceeded to the United States of America.

She had planned to start a private school when she returned from the United States. Her last desire would be to see her school suffer bouts of inferiority due to unpreparedness from the older ones that were adequately funded and with good infrastructures. She hoped to have her school properly furnished and equipped at the cradle and kindergarten levels. There would be cribs, big play grounds, swings and other types of outdoor items. She would need other educational materials and aids for the primary levels like, computers, white boards, overhead projectors, water fountains or dispensers, video cameras, furniture, the list was endless. The building had to meet with the standards of the city. Her projection was to start with a hundred children next academic season and that would make a lot of difference. She had also put in application for the school to become a center for local, national and some international examinations. She thought that her visit to America would make a lot of difference. She needed nursery books for the library and she hoped to get them. Ify was very optimistic.

The flight was about six hours to Holland and another nine to Houston, Texas. Big Cousin's wife, Anna, was at the airport to receive Ify. The first sight that held her captive was the size of the Americans. They were enormous and rode in very large vehicles. Ify had never seen people of these sizes. The rich people and the opulent were associated with large body sizes in the part of the world she came from. These ones with massive bodies must be very rich, she thought.

The airport was another wonder to behold. There was brilliant light everywhere. The passengers and relations kissed and hugged each other. The atmosphere was charged with laughter. She felt a big burden lifted from her shoulders, like a bird released from captivity. Her destiny was being fulfilled. She recognized that this was the country she had been dreaming to visit. She observed very beautiful scenes as they drove to Anna and Big Cousin's home in another part of the town. She saw well-designed homes, bridges crisscrossing each other, and big cars. They shone with powerful brilliance. What she witnessed was not to be compared with the stories she heard. This was the wealthiest nation on planet Earth. It was the "American wonder." She could hear the good old song that the village magician was always singing:

> Come and see the American wonder
>
> Come and see the American wonder
>
> Come and see the American wonder
>
> Come and see the American wonder.

She and Anna drove the few miles to Cedar Hill. Anna and Big Cousin had been married since 1977 and had five children.

The first vacation that Ify took was in Big Cousin's apartment, two years after their marriage. Anna was a typical village wife any husband would be proud of. She was the favorite of the family. While the family members crucified Big Cousin, Anna received endless praises. Her mother had given her good home training. Ify continued in her wild thoughts. What would this country hold for her? Were the people as beautiful as the city looked? Were they friendly like the people she had been used to? Only time would tell.

Her routine was to stay home the whole day, sleeping or eating or watching the television. It was a three-bedroom home. The youngest two girls were still in high school. They were large, like the other citizens of the country. Ify wondered why there were so many huge people everywhere. She had never seen such sizes in her life. They were everywhere. If she turned here, they were there; she turned there, they were there. They all drove in huge vehicles. She used to see herself as a chubby woman, but now her size was not to be compared to the large people she saw. She recalled that her last vacation in France was so frustrating because she found it hard to find clothes of her size. The major boutiques had little sizes that didn't fit her. In the end, she had to give up and was satisfied with the used clothes she purchased in the Sunday flea market. All the stores in America had her size. It could not be compared with her last visit to France, where she combed the major stores without finding her sizes.

One day her younger cousin, Monday, called. He had asked her to get hold of his girlfriend who was staying in Dallas for assistance in shopping because Aunty Anna spent so much time at work. Ify was getting ready to return after her long vacation. That was a turning point in her life. Her cousin's girlfriend's name was Stella-Maris. She was just like the Americans. Ify came to the conclusion that food must be no problem here when she saw the sizes of both men and women. It was not like home. Fatness was a result of genetic tendencies or associated with opulence and not found as easily—or at least not the huge sizes she saw in comparison in America. Anna had cautioned her to always look away anytime she saw large people, but she found it to be so hard. She continued to wonder why there were so many people like that. It couldn't be food, she concluded. Anyway, Ify held her breath as Stella walked toward her with open arms. Despite her size, she was very warm hearted, and that was a consolation for Ify.

They drove for another thirty minutes before they arrived in her apartment. It was two bedrooms. Stella and her son shared a room. The second room was bare, with cartons of old shoes littering the floor. Ify's bed for the next six weeks was to be the sofa in the living room. The other choice, which she discovered the best, was to spread the thick comforter on the floor and lay on it.

Stella was kind hearted and showed much concern for Ify. Ify was glad to find someone to talk to and more so was glad that the apartment's location was in the center of the town. Stella was not new to the country. She had her university education in accounting and was a citizen. Her son was in kindergarten. They got along well enough. They went shopping, swimming, and dining. They had much fun until Ify returned home

She looked through the little window as the plane taxied on the tarmac, getting ready to make the final halt. She dipped her hand into her breast pocket and brought out a little poem she had composed in praise of the most blessed and wonderful nation on the face of the planet, God's own country and the last Paradise.

Amérique Mon Amérique!

Terres des Prairies, Pouvoir, et Pens;

Beaute du Pain, de la beurre, du miel;

Nids d'amours, amitiés et démons;

Ouvert aux jeunes et des vieux;

Dieu, Or, Pistolets sur les Rues;

Berceau en farveur depuis de la création:

Paradis Perdu! Je t'aime! La défense d'Israël!

The End

Moral Relevance of the Tales

(Other meanings may also apply)

Mama and the Pot of Egusi Soup

Man should dwell in unity, devoid of ethnic, tribal, or racial differences. God is a God of purpose and full of love. When we come together and are united, we will overcome and victory is sure. Men ought to live and love one another.

The Uncrowned King

God has instructed parents to train up their children in the admonition of the Lord, so that when they grow, they will not depart from it. A foolish child will bring sorrow to the parents because he/she is a symbol of the training received. No child should be bigger than his/her parents for discipline.

The Scorpion and the Tortoise

We should be careful of unfriendly friends who appear in sheep's clothing. They look for any opportunity to destroy. The Holy Bible has taught us that the thief has come to steal, kill, and destroy. We need a discerning spirit to know who our true friends are.

The Hunter and the Palm Kernel

Never give up, even when you are faced with poor odds. Whose report shall we believe? Certainly it's the Lord's. Our thinking should be positive at all times.

Onwuero

Pride goes before a fall. Those who lack wisdom should ask for it, and God will give it. A stubborn fly will follow the corpse into the ground. Girls, listen to your parents and pray that God will order your steps.

The Coral Beads

The wicked shall perish in their wickedness. God abhors wickedness with perfect hatred. We must shun all appearances of evil. God is loving and forgiving. It's by His mercy that man is not consumed. Forgiveness is godliness.

All of You

Everything is vanity. The Bible teaches that the lover of silver will never be satisfied. We must shun greed and bless God for the little that we have. We must love our neighbors as we love ourselves.

The Beaded Necklace

A child who is ill bred will pull down his father's dynasty when he inherits it. A foolish child will bring sorrow to his father.

Why Men Have Catarrh

Let wisdom prevail in all things. We must never take things for granted. The devil is out there looking for someone he can devour.

Why Men Don't Have Tails

God has given unto man many gifts and talents. They must be used to bring glory to His name.

Dike the Great Wrestler

God is the author and the finisher of our faith. Woe to him who depends on the arms of flesh, for they will utterly fail. God is the rock of our salvation, and in Him we have our being. We can do all things through Christ who strengthens us.

A Dance in the Forest

God is the father of the orphan. He is the defender of the weak. His eyes roam to and fro in search of His children because they are the apples of His eyes. He will never allow those who trust in Him to suffer any shame. The wicked shall perish in their wickedness.

Glossary

1. Dodo: a staple food among the Caribbean and black Africans made from plantains. It is similar to bananas.
2. Oseani: a kind of soup made with roots and herbs and no oil.
3. Egusi: soup made with melon seeds.
4. Agbona: a kind of soup like okra, rich in cholesterol.
5. Orie: market day
6. Igbankwu wanyi: Customary marriage introduction ceremony.
7. Jollof: Tomato-colored rice
8. Ifeanyinachukwu: With God, nothing shall be impossible.
9. Nkwo: market day
10. Kano fish: fired fish from the northern state of Kano.
11. Koboko: horse whip
12. Tayintayin: tooth picker
13. Akara: bean balls
14. Ewa: beauty

15. Moinmoin: pudding made from bean paste.
16. Ogi: paste from corn.
17. Puff-puff: similar to donuts
18. Gari: cassava flour
19. Na wa o: an expression of surprise
20. Obi: chief or king or head of the town
21. Ogogoro: local gin or illicit alcohol
22. Onwuero: song

> Please return to your mother;
> Our home is in the deep:
> The waters are deep;
> The deep is deadly:
> Fish live in the deep.
> Dolphins are fish that live in the deep;
> The catfish also live in the deep:
> Sea pythons are fish that live in the deep;
> The deep is deadly;
> Fish live in the deep and not in homes;
> The world is nothing but vanity.

23. Edumare: God, almighty
24. Nene: darling
25. Inokpor: native waist band
26. Her flower: menstrual period
27. Amerique mon Amerique:

America, My America

Land of great prairies, power, and pen
Beauty, bread, butter, and honey;
Nesting friends and fiends;
Opportunity to old and young;
God, gold, gun on streets;
Cradle favored at creation;
Lost paradise, how I want you, Israel's shield.

CPSIA information can be obtained at www.ICGtesting.com
Printed in the USA
LVOW130133260613

340206LV00002B/2/P